HERB'S PAJAMAS

HERB'S PAJAMAS

ABIGAIL **THOMAS**

ALGONQUIN BOOKS OF CHAPEL HILL **1998**

Published by
ALGONQUIN BOOKS OF CHAPEL HILL
Post Office Box 2225
Chapel Hill, North Carolina 27515-2225

a division of
WORKMAN PUBLISHING
708 Broadway
New York, New York 10003

Grateful acknowledgment is made to the magazines and periodicals that originally published several of these short stories, some in a slightly different form: *East Hampton Star* ("Negligee"), *Ms.* ("Shoes," published as "Here"), and *Glimmer Train* ("Herb's Pajamas").

This is a work of fiction. While, as in all fiction, the literary perceptions and insights are based on experience, all names, characters, places, and incidents are either products of the author's imagination or are used fictitiously. No references to any real person is intended or should be inferred.

LIBRARY OF CONGRESS CATALOGING-IN-PUBLICATION DATA
Thomas, Abigail.
    Herb's pajamas / Abigail Thomas.
        p.   cm.
    ISBN 1-56512-189-9
    1. Manhattan (New York, N.Y.)—Social life and customs—Fiction.
    2. City and town life—New York (State)—New York—Fiction.
    I. Title.
PS3570.H53H47   1998
813'.54—dc21   97-32433
                                                            CIP

10 9 8 7 6 5 4 3 2 1

FIRST EDITION

THANKS TO ALL THE USUAL SUSPECTS: my brilliant editor, Shannon Ravenel; Chuck Verrill and Liz Darhansoff (whom I live to please); my daughters Sarah, Jennifer, Catherine; my son, Ralph; my sisters Judy and Eliza. My husband Rich. My mother. Special thanks to Quin Luttinger, old friend, whose wonderful story gave Walter meaning and purpose. And last but not least, thanks to the Tuesday Night Babes, who have enriched my life in more ways than could ever have been reasonably expected.

FOR RICH, WITH GRATITUDE AND LOVE

CONTENTS

WALTER'SBOOK 1

EDITH'SWARDROBE 45

   HATS **47**

   NEGLIGEE **53**

   GLOVES **62**

   HANDKERCHIEFS **66**

   FUR COAT **72**

   LEOPARD-SKIN SKIRT **82**

   TOTES **87**

   FIG LEAF **91**

   SUNGLASSES **94**

   SHOES **96**

   SHOPPING BAG **109**

   BIRTHDAY SUIT **111**

   UNDERWEAR **113**

   NO POCKETBOOK **120**

BUNNY'SSISTER **123**

HERB'SPAJAMAS **189**

WALTER'SBOOK

WALTER STANDS IN front of the open icebox. He peers inside, leaning down for the milk. It is three-thirty in the morning. Closing the icebox door, Walter shuffles over to the cupboard and reaches for the cereal box (left-hand corner, bottom shelf), pivots to take a bowl (blue with a single chip) out of the dish rack, then stands at the counter and assembles a helping of cornflakes. He does all this in the dark. Then he sits down to have what he calls his breakfast. "It's not called breakfast in the middle of the night, Dad," Julie has pointed out to him. "It's called insomnia."

Walter doesn't think so. Insomnia is where you can't get to sleep at all. Walter can get to sleep all right, he just can't stay asleep. One minute he's out cold, the next he's staring at the ceiling. Walter is fifty-five; at his age you probably need less sack time. He should really use these hours to work, but instead he goes padding around in the dark. He's proud of being able to get through the tricky living room without knocking into anything, without tripping over the footstool; he loves knowing exactly when to put his right hand down to brush the worn velvet of his old red couch. He loves negotiating the long dark hall and knowing where to turn left for the kitchen. He loves the odd sparks his hand makes in the dark when it connects with the icebox handle.

Walter munches away now, spoonful after spoonful, his head full of the details of cereal. It takes a full two minutes for the texture of cornflakes to change from crisp to soggy, Walter knows, and he has never minded soggy. Soggy has its own virtues, he maintains, and tonight when he has eaten the last delicious spoonful (gritty with sugar) he sighs, and gets up to rinse the bowl. Then he stands in front of the kitchen window. A southern exposure. Most of the city is dark. Walter looks down at the fourth floor across the street, where there are always lights burning in the third window from the left. "It's a plant light, Dad," Julie has said, but Walter doesn't think so. He senses a kindred soul. He stands there some minutes, like a wading bird, on one leg. Then he turns and heads back to bed.

It is easier on the way back, his eyes accustomed to the darkness.

TONIGHT THERE IS a thin bar of light under his daughter's door. He doesn't want to notice, but he does. It was there last night too, and when he knocked it was instantly extinguished. Tonight he hesitates, then knocks gently. The light stays on and he takes this as a sign to knock again, which he does, and pushes the door open. The air is filled with cigarette smoke, layer upon layer, like stratus clouds, which the opening door disturbs.

"Julie?"

"Hi, Dad." Julie is sitting by the window. She looks small, too small to smoke so much, that's what Walter is dying to say. She was supposed to be quitting. She and her mother were both quitting together. Ellie told him last week.

"Smoky in here." Walter pretends to do the breast-stroke. He can see a half-eaten Peppermint Pattie on the arm of her chair.

"Very funny, Dad." She is only half turned toward him. She has been looking out the window, the curtains are open. The sky is a violet black, very beautiful. Somewhere a red beacon goes on, off, and Walter can make out the dark shape of a water tower impossibly visible against the night sky. What a beautiful city this is, thinks Walter for the millionth time.

"You all right? It's four in the morning."

"I'm fine, Dad." She smiles at him.

"But you're up."

"I'm up." Julie stubs out a cigarette. "So are you."

"I had a little cereal."

"I know, Dad. Breakfast." On Julie's bedside table (painted red, decals of Dumbo and Bambi unsuccessfully scraped off the left-hand corner) are three more Peppermint Patties (a passion she shares with her mother) and a teacup half full of tea in which float several cigarette butts.

"That's disgusting," he says, grimacing at the cup. "That alone should persuade you to quit."

"Right."

"Why are you up? Everything okay?"

"Insomnia, Dad. Don't look so worried. I probably got it from you."

"Is your mother aware of this?" Walter asks. He would like to hug her but settles for resting his hand on the back of her chair.

"Aware of what."

"Of your being up at night a lot."

"She knows." Julie is lighting matches now, and letting them burn down to her fingertips. He wishes she would stop.

"What does she do?"

"She makes me hot milk. No, Dad, don't. Really. Please don't. I'm fine, really." Julie takes half a cigarette out of her pocket and lights it carefully. She is wearing Ellie's fuzzy old pink chenille bathrobe. It is ratty and soft and sometimes when neither his daughter nor his former wife is around Walter sleeps with it in the bed next to him.

"I thought you were quitting," he says, unable to help himself. "You and your mother both."

"Mom hasn't had a cigarette in five days," says Julie briefly. She blows a smoke ring and tucks a strand of hair back off her face. Her dark eyebrows, more startling than usual, remind him of the spread wings of some ocean-going bird. It always amazes him how beautiful his child is.

"You know all the carcinogens are in the part closest to the filter." Walter can't help himself.

"Really." She taps the cigarette against the side of the ashtray, looking up at him curiously.

"So if you're going to smoke half, why not the first half?" Walter's hands are now hanging at his sides.

"I did smoke the first half, Dad," says Julie conversationally. "Now I'm smoking the second."

There seems no good answer to this.

"Dad, I'm pooped. Let's go to bed. You go to bed, okay?"

"All right then," says Walter, but he makes no move to leave. "Think that's the bridge?" he says finally. He is looking at the red beacon way uptown.

"Go to bed, Pop."

Walter, heartened by her use of the word "Pop," bends down to kiss the top of her head. "You're sure there's nothing I can do?"

"Nope," says Julie. She turns back to the window. Walter is uncomfortable just leaving her there like that.

"I thought you were going to bed," he says, hesitating at the door.

"Dad," she says firmly. "Sweet dreams."

"Sweet dreams," says Walter. "Sweet dreams."

But Walter cannot sleep. He lies on his back, his side, his stomach. He sits on the edge of the bed. He recites "Dover Beach," the first poem he learned by heart. Dawn surprises him an hour later, the sun rising beautifully red over Queens.

LAST WEEK WALTER'S former wife, Ellie, had spent the night. Julie was due back from school for a spring break and Ellie had turned up out of the blue with an armful of Julie's spring clothes. Walter had been reading the newspaper when the doorbell rang. "It's me, Ellie!" she had shouted into the phone downstairs, and he had buzzed her up, straightening his tie in the mirror and brushing back his hair with the palm of his hand before answering the door. It was the third time she'd dropped by in three weeks. She had seemed nervous when she came in, and had sat down abruptly on the couch. He had sat opposite her in the yellow chair, his hands on his knees.

"Walter," she had begun, "I think we should talk."

"Yes, Ellie?" he had said, leaning forward perhaps a bit too eagerly. She seemed lonely, he had thought perhaps she was coming back. Perhaps he had smiled too quickly, because her mood had changed. Instead of talking, she had picked up a black clam shell from the coffee table.

"You still have this?" Picking it up and turning it over in her hand.

"Of course I do," he had said.

"And this too?" She had held up a windshield wiper, flattened into the shape, she had once thought, of a flying bird. She had picked it out of the gutter on Broadway herself, twenty years ago. He had nodded. She was looking around the living room as if she hadn't seen it a million times over the last twenty-some years. "Walter, everything looks just the same as it did when I moved out."

"Yes," he had agreed, "I suppose it does."

"Doesn't that seem strange?"

"Everything is how I like it, Ellie, I'm comfortable here. This is my home." And yours too, if you want it, he had forborne saying.

She had stood up and said, "What's in the kitchen. I'm hungry."

She had stayed for supper. Made supper, even. She had fussed a lot ("Is this what you call a chicken?" "How old is this rosemary?" "Have you no fresh garlic, for god sake?"), but he had thoroughly enjoyed it. He knew she was in a good mood when she bossed him around. ("Get me a sharp knife, no, a clean sharp knife, hand me a bunch of that flour, please,what? Is this all the flour? Don't tell me!") He had loved every minute of it. Fuss, flour on the floor, the smell of oil and butter smoking on the stove. The hiss and sizzle of delicious things hitting a hot frying pan. Ellie exclaiming on the sorry state of his kitchen floor (mopped that very morning) and refusing to touch his dish towels. He had stayed in the kitchen and watched her cook, his hands behind his back, while she frowned and measured and threw things together. Then they had eaten the chicken she had invented (using honey and soy sauce and an ancient bottle of horseradish) and it had been delicious. After supper they had watched a *Star Trek* rerun sitting on the red velvet sofa side by side (Walter holding his breath) and then she'd asked him questions.

"Have you gone out at all in the last six months?"

"You mean out out? As in with a woman?" He had shaken his head. "Why would I do that?" He had been genuinely bewildered.

"I was just wondering. I think you need to see more people. You know. Have a date or something." She'd patted his hand. He had withdrawn it.

"I have what I need," he had said. "Really." It had seemed to him something was right on the tip of Ellie's tongue, but "Oh, Walter" was all she'd said. Then when the thunderstorm had broken Ellie had looked dubiously out the window. "Why don't you spend the night, Ellie," Walter had suggested, and at first she had hesitated. But rain had spattered against the windows, the wind had howled, thunder had crashed, and Ellie had said she would, if it was really all right with him. She would sleep on the couch if he still had the old army blanket.

"Nonsense," he had answered.

Five minutes later, teeth brushed, nightclothes donned (Ellie in a pair of his pajamas), they had stood next to the bed together. "*I* can sleep on the couch, Ellie, if you'd be more comfortable," said Walter. He'd been oh so aware of his wife's body in his old pajamas, her breath smelling of toothpaste.

"Don't be ridiculous, Walt, this is your house," she'd said. That was disappointing, the way she'd said "your house" like that. But he'd loved having her there, heaped up like a small warm sand dune beside him. It had seemed a long time before her breathing was regular. "Ellie?" he had ventured once. "Are you awake?" but she hadn't answered. In the morning he had woken first, and turned his head to look at her. Didn't she know how good this was? How right they were together? Look at how relaxed she looked sleeping in their bed again. He'd spent a moment adjusting his breathing to match hers. Then, on sudden inspiration, he had gotten up quickly and quietly and made real coffee, not just instant. Ten minutes later she'd appeared in the kitchen, all dressed, just as he was about to break eggs into a bowl. He had set the table with napkins and everything.

"French toast, how does that sound?" He'd been smiling.

"Oh, god, Walter," she'd said, clearly upset, " I wish you hadn't done this. I should never have spent the night." He had been bewildered and disappointed. "You know I love you, Walter, but we need to talk." He had nodded his head. "Of course, Ellie, of course," and then she'd left quickly and he could hear her through the front door as she waited for the elevator saying, "God, god, god, god, god."

WALTER RIDES THE subway this morning, he wants to surprise Julie with chocolate croissants from Zabar's. The train is crowded but at Ninety-sixth it clears out and Walter finds a seat next to an old man who is writing laboriously in a tattered blue notebook. Walter glances over. The headline at the top of the page reads "A Brief Description of My Pain." Walter is moved to continue. "I have pain and swiftness in my lower back and it shoots down my left buttock." Walter looks more closely at the man. He is obviously poor: the large toe of his left foot has worn a hole in the canvas shoes he wears and the knees of his old trousers are stained. The collar of his shirt is frayed and the cuffs torn. There is grime in the seams of his neck. But his face shines with the dignity of concentration. Walter marvels at his use of the words "swiftness" and "buttock." "It is also in my left calf," Walter continues reading, "also the three toes of my left foot are numb." Beyond that Walter cannot read, the man's arm covers his page as he thinks. There is a kind of holiness in his accuracy, thinks Walter, a kind of faith. This man believes in something.

My wife has left me, thinks Walter. My child doesn't sleep. There is pain and swiftness in my life.

He hardly noticed it at first, just a tingling in his extremities. It was even somewhat pleasurable, at least for a while. After a couple of hours, though, as the intensity of the sensation increased, he became frightened.

Walter puts down his pen. It is late morning, Julie is still asleep. Chocolate croissants sit on a plate on the kitchen table. Walter's study is lined with books. A bookcase is as good as a fireplace, he has always thought. He sits in his old Morris chair, pissed on once (maybe more than once) by an old tomcat Julie had rescued from the wilds of Riverside Park twelve years ago. They had kept it three days. No doubt he should be attending to the stack of manuscripts (Walter is a copy editor for a textbook publisher; his specialty is children's math workbooks, grades one through seven) but instead Walter leans his head back, gazing at the ceiling. On damp days the old chair still smells. Who was it that kept a basket of fermenting apples under his desk? He closes his eyes, then picks up his pen again, adjusting the long yellow pad on his knee.

So when the voice spoke in his mind he was almost relieved.

IT: *You have nothing to fear, I'm a Superior Being that just has a momentary need of your body and brain. I will relinquish them in due course and undamaged.*

HE: *And when might that be?*

IT: *Perhaps a few years, perhaps a few days, who knows.*

HE: *Will the numbness and tingling continue as long as you're here?*

IT: *Yes, since I need a little more power than your nervous system can supply, but I believe that you'll get used to it. Forgive me now if I temporarily discontinue this interesting chat, but I have things to do that require attention.*

Where was all this coming from? Ellie had asked him about the new book and he'd said it was going well. It was going well. But what was it? How could this be happening, the voices in his head?

He found that although his body had not moved he seemed to be on a beach, and it was a warm sunny summer day. After a few moments he realized that he was remembeing a period early in his marriage, when he had loved that beach,

*those summers. He found that he could move the scene a bit
up and down the shore. Suddenly, miraculously, there was his
daughter, aged about four, talking to the waves. And there
was his wife, her black hair in thick curls around her face,
wearing her yellow bathing suit. She was saying something
that he could not quite hear. The whole scene, the sky, the
sun, the water, seemed to freeze into a radiant timelessness.*

Then the voice came on again.

IT: *Sorry to leave you alone for so long, but it was necessary.
Did you like the memory?*

Walter puts his pen down again and blows his nose,
wipes his eyes.

ELLIE MOVED THE furniture around a lot in the weeks before she left. Walter would come home and find the couch
in the middle of the room and the television in the closet.
"What's going on?" he'd call out jovially, "Where is everything?" and Ellie would fly off the handle. "I didn't mean
to criticize," he'd say. But he remembers the look of un-
certainty on her face and within hours she'd have moved
everything back. Then for a while she had wanted to
move out of the city altogether. Maybe even out of the
state. "Julie's in college," she'd said, "we're free to move if
we want. We've been in this apartment for twenty years
now, Walter." He had let her wear herself out on that one.

"Come look with me," she'd said, and he had gone to oblige her. "It's very nice. But don't you think you would be bored? Grass is just grass, after all, Ellie, but the city is different every minute. Did you notice the mildew on the floorboards by the sink in the bathroom?"

One day she had stopped talking about it.

JULIE IS AWAKE now. He can hear the bedroom door opening and the bathroom door closing and the muffled sound of a radio playing rock 'n' roll. The hiss of the shower. Those exhilarating signs of life. Walter loves the sounds of his daughter rising. Sometimes he can even (through some accident of acoustics), hear her metal hangers scrape in the closet while she decides what to wear. Now she is moving around in the kitchen. He hears a cupboard open and close, dishes being set down, drawers being shut. The fridge opens and closes twice. He doesn't want to hover. No point in crowding her. "Dad?" she calls, and he is out of his chair like a shot.

"Welcome to the land of the living." Walter enters smiling but he is dismayed to see a cigarette in her hand. "You're smoking." She is sitting in her old spot on the radiator.

"Dad. You're so observant." She crosses her legs and tilts her head the way she always does when she gets ready to talk. "The first one always gives me an anxiety attack," she explains. "I have to get it over with fast." Her hair is newly washed and combed but she is still in her bathrobe. "Hey, thanks for the croissants. You went to so much trouble, Dad."

Walter beams. There is no detectable edge in Julie's voice this morning. Walter thinks maybe it would be safe to ask a few questions, draw her out a little. Of course, he must proceed cautiously.

"How are you feeling?" A nice slow beginning.

"Fine." Julie blows a smoke ring. "How about you?"

"Fine. Tea this morning?" he asks and she nods.

"Thanks. Tea is great."

He puts a tea bag in one mug and measures instant coffee into another. The flame is already on under the kettle and he picks it up to make sure there is enough water inside. "Not much sleep, right?" Walter fills the sugar bowl and finds a clean spoon. Just the gentlest of probes.

"Dad, I'm fine."

"If anything is bothering you, you know your old dad is here to listen."

"Thanks, Dad. I appreciate it."

"Because you've seemed a bit down in the mouth of late. Up at night and so forth."

"Sometimes a person has to think things through alone. You understand that, don't you? Some things are hard to talk about." She reaches into her pocket for a comb and combs her hair straight back from her face, her eyes half-closing as she does so. Such a graceful gesture. Sometimes she reminds him so much of her mother.

"Of course, of course." Walter pours the water into the cups. "How about sugar?" Julie shakes her head. He drops two spoonsful of sugar into his coffee, then brings both cups to the table and sits down. "What things? Think what things through?" It is like a tic, fatherhood.

Julie rolls her eyes, swinging her legs back to the floor. "I'm going to get dressed, Dad. Thanks for the tea." But she leaves it on the table. After a moment Walter stands up, pours his coffee away, and rinses the mug. He puts the croissants back in the bag and folds it up tight, leaving it out on the table. He doesn't know what to do about her tea.

Ten minutes later Julie comes back. Walter is standing in front of the window, lost in thought. Well, maybe not thought exactly, more like the absence of thought.

"Hi," she says, and kisses his cheek. "Are you going to this? It's tonight." She is holding an invitation in her hand. She sits on the radiator again.

Walter looks at it and shakes his head. "I never go to reunions."

"Why not?"

He shrugs. "I just don't."

"You can't stay cooped up here for the rest of your life."

"I'm not cooped up. This is my home. My castle."

"But listen, Dad, it might be fun."

"I don't want to have fun," he says. "I have plenty of fun."

"It would be like an adventure, Dad. Really. I think you should go."

"I don't want an adventure, Jule," he says. "I like my life the way it is."

Julie points to the icebox. "Dad, listen to me. You know what's in there? Same old stuff. You eat the same stuff. You eat it off the same plate. You use the exact same knife and fork every night and then you wash it and put it away. You don't even use different cups in the morning. You don't call anybody, you don't see anybody."

Walter speaks after a pause. "At my age I have habits." He would like to add something to that, but nothing comes to mind.

"Why don't you go?" Julie stands with her arms folded. "What possible harm could it do you to go?" He mumbles something noncommital.

"What?"

"I said I haven't seen these people in thirty years."

"You haven't seen any people, Pop. You don't even go three blocks in either direction."

"That's just not true. I went to Zabar's this morning," says Walter.

"You're a hermit, Dad," says Julie.

"I'm not a hermit. I'm a recluse." He looks at her but she isn't smiling. "I go out. I take walks."

"Walks don't cut it, Dad. You need to see people."

"I do see people. I will be seeing Grandma this afternoon. Have you spoken to your mother today?" asks Walter, changing the subject.

"No." Julie shakes her head with vehemence.

"You know your mother came here last week and we had a nice meal together. I don't know whether she mentioned it to you. It was just before you came back for spring break." His heart is beating fast for no reason. "She wound up spending the night. There was a bad storm. I believe we will be having a drink together this afternoon." Walter searches his daughter's face for clues but Julie is frowning. "I wonder if your mother isn't a little lonely."

Julie gets off the radiator and stands next to him at the kitchen window. Walter puts his arm around her shoulders. "I love you, Dad," she says, and buries her face in his shirt.

"Well of course you do, Julie," he says, surprised at her tears. "I wouldn't have it any other way." He smooths her hair as she cries against him. "I love you too, Julie, what's the matter. Tell your old daddy, maybe I can help."

She shakes her head and dries her eyes on her bathrobe. She points down at the seedy hotel across the street.

"They're out again. Look. Your favorites." She smiles at him. "I've got to blow my nose," she says, and hurries down the hall. Walter looks back out the window, where several men have come out on the roof. They are Mexicans, Walter thinks. Or maybe Guatemalans. They have guitars with them, and they are dragging their painted chairs.

ELLIE NEVER SAID she'd been unhappy. She had always seemed happy, or at least happy enough. Whatever happiness was, and Walter found he wasn't sure himself. Certainly nothing you could pursue. Anyway, it wasn't happiness she'd been after, she had made that much clear. She wanted to be alone, that was all. "I want to be alone. I have never done anything by myself." Sometimes she said it with an accent, like Greta Garbo. But that was before it had gathered its full head of steam.

"I'll rent an office," said Walter at first, while Ellie's tone was still apologetic. "I'll get out of your hair. You can be alone all day long." But that was not what she meant. "How about vacation? Take a trip by yourself somewhere?" Ellie shook her head.

"I just want to be by myself, Walt, I can't explain it." Walter could hardly hear her.

"Can we rent you a cottage for the summer? You go by yourself and I won't come unless you invite me?" She shook her head again, it was so difficult to know what she really meant.

"I don't want to feel guilty thinking about you waiting by the phone," she began softly. They were sitting in the kitchen. Walter was still in his bathrobe and slippers. He looked down at the tablecloth. This foolish tablecloth he had given her on her fortieth birthday, the map of Hawaii, where they had never been but jokingly planned to retire. "Only twenty-five years until Aloha," Walter's card had read.

"I just want to be by myself, Walt. I can't explain it."

He leaned forward. "Is there something I'm doing wrong?" Walter's throat was tight. "Something I could do better?" And here he felt Ellie soften, as if she might have fallen weeping into his arms, but instead she pushed her chair back and stood up. It was one of those moments where life could go either way.

"No, Walter. It's me. There's something wrong with me." She ran her hands through her hair. Ellie's skin was always very white, even in summer. White skin, dark, dark hair. His beautiful wife. Drifting away. Out of reach.

"For how long?" Walter asked.

"I don't know. I really don't know." She tried to smile at him.

"A month?" She couldn't meet his eyes. "More than a month?"

Ellie didn't answer. She picked up a book. She touched its spine. She put it down.

"How long, Ellie. I deserve an answer."

"There's a sublet in the Village. A year."

"A year!"

"But I don't know if that's how long," she added. "I might be home next weekend, who knows, with my tail between my legs."

"What about the child?"

"She's in college, Walt. We'll still be her parents. But she's getting to be her own self now. Besides. It might not be forever. Think of it as a vacation." She smiled again, weakly. "A vacation from the harridan."

"I don't want a vacation," Walter said, as close to raising his voice as he had ever gotten. "You are my vacation."

"I need to do something else. I can't stay here another second," she said, beginning to cry.

"You're not my vacation, Ellie," Walter amended, patting her back as she leaned against his shoulder." You're my whole life."

But that was even worse.

He had gone away the day before Ellie packed up, unable to watch her fill the boxes, unable to bear the excitement she couldn't hide. She hadn't even taken much. Her clothes. Her bureau swept clean of clutter. Two years ago now. And where did she go? Not the deserts of Arizona, not an abandoned dairy farm in Pennsylvania, not an orchard in upstate New York. She went downtown to Bleecker Street, an apartment across from a butcher shop with rabbits hanging upside down in its windows.

ELLIE ANSWERS THE phone on the third ring.

"Hello?"

"Ellie, it's me, Walter."

"Yes. I recognized your voice, Walt." Is she laughing at him? It is unnerving the way women find things funny.

"Are we getting together today?"

"We are, Walt. This afternoon."

"I wasn't sure if I had the time right."

"Five okay?"

"Perfect." So he hadn't dreamed it. "Is everything all right?"

"I'm okay, Walt." Her voice has such a strange note in it.

"Because I'm worried about Julie."

Silence.

"She seems so unlike herself. Cranky and so forth. Have you noticed anything?"

"She's nineteen, Walter. Old enough to have her own problems."

"But what could be wrong? I wondered if you had any insights."

"Whatever it is, Walt, she'll either tell you about it or

she won't. That's about all I can say." Ellie's voice has that dreadful curtness in it.

"Well," he finishes up, "I will see you this afternoon." Three seconds later the phone rings. It is Ellie again.

"I'm sorry for being so short."

"That's all right," says Walter, but he is wary, like a burn victim.

"We'll talk later, Walt." Her voice is gentle, gentler than he has ever heard it before.

Walter hangs up with a nervous feeling in the pit of his stomach.

IT: *I'm sorry, I was distracted for a moment. Did you like the memory?*

HE: *It was lovely but somewhat melancholy for me and I would prefer not to discuss it. Would it be impertinent of me to ask you some questions about yourself, your purpose here, and things in general?*

IT: *Well, not exactly impertinent, but to a Superior Being like myself a dialogue with a being of your kind has only very limited interest. But you may begin.*

HE: *So first, what sort of thing are you?*

IT: *Oh, well, it's a little hard to explain what I am in terms you could understand. My sort evolved—though under very different conditions—as yours did, from the organic world. But after a while our command of science enabled us to shed our biological forms and transform ourselves into almost invulnerable machines. Marvelous as they were—they had powerful bodies and minds, and a great emotional range—we found them limiting in the long run, and it became our principal goal to free our Selves from the bondage of a material body. Finally what was achieved was a purely mental Entity that could control any organic or inorganic machine in any way consistent with the machine's construction. I am such an entity. Each of us is an individual, subject only to its own needs and purposes.*

HE: I am very curious to know what those needs and what those purposes might be. But before that, tell me, are you subject to the laws of nature as we know them, or can you do anything?

Eleven o'clock now. Walter is walking down Broadway, past the Cathedral Market with its bins of fruits and vegetables, past the old Woolworth's, which somehow manages to hold its own amidst the cropping up of new sneaker stores and Radio Shacks and discount drugstores. He still has more than an hour before he is due at his mother's, not that time matters to his mother, but Walter likes to be prompt. Perhaps he will drop in at the bookstore. Visit his book. He seems to be going in that direction anyway. Maybe it's silly, he thinks, pausing outside the New Delhi Restaurant, under the tattered little plastic banners announcing its opening. But some days there are two copies, then other days there are four, then three days later only one. It must be selling nicely, wonder of wonders. And where it had come from, who knew? A kind of miracle. Three years ago he had sat down with the window open and pen and paper and it had more or less appeared on the page. Six months later he'd sent it off and sold it right away. "Dear Mr. Wilson" (the letter had read), "Who are you?" They'd offered him a modest sum and lots of enthusiasm. A sci-fi fairy tale, was how they'd sold it.

Walter walks purposefully the rest of the way to the Single Woman's Bookstore, so named because a single woman owns and runs it, the heiress to some large fortune, or so Walter assumes. Cooking oil? Department stores? When she first opened the store she served coffee and tiny sandwiches but there are no longer such niceties. Georgia has recently given birth to a son. She is nursing her infant behind the cash register when Walter pushes open the door this morning, the bell tinkling pleasantly as he enters.

"Hello again," she says cheerfully.

"Hello," he says cautiously, "pleasant day out there."

He isn't always certain he wants to hear what Georgia has to say, she is not a shy woman. Lorenzo, it seems, is the pink result of a one-afternoon stand with a young Con Ed worker who had winked at her. "Want to fuck?" she'd asked him. Walter had blushed the first time Georgia spoke about herself. "Theoretically, this was an immaculate conception," she'd confided, "in that he was conceived in the shower. Well, perhaps not immaculate per se, but very, very clean. We had it on lukewarm because I know what hot does to a guy's sperm count. Momma didn't want a soft-boiled egg. She wanted Lorenzo, didn't she, angel-face," she'd continued, planting a kiss on the baby's head. It was perhaps more than Walter needed to know. Walter was almost afraid to ask what had happened to the young man.

"Where is the father?" he finally did inquire, curiosity getting the better of him.

"Tom? Oh, I ate him," said Georgia, laughing.

Today Lorenzo nurses, Georgia's bosom half covered by a green shawl. These sounds of contentment are the most beautiful in the world, thinks Walter, the sounds of a small creature being filled to the very top with milk.

"He's getting big, isn't he," says Walter.

"Momma's boy," says Georgia. "He has no choice."

Walter turns away, planning to drift toward the science-fiction shelves, when Georgia speaks. "Want to hold him for me a sec? I've got to stick a quarter in my meter." And before Walter has a chance to answer she walks over and thrusts the little creature into his arms.

Walter has forgotten how nice a baby feels against the

shoulder, the sweet warm weight, the look of the pursed lips swollen to a pink, impossibly thin blister by suckling. He smiles, Lorenzo in his arms, the baby's warm breath against the side of his neck, he can feel the tiny exhalations. Good Lord, thinks Walter. He walks back and forth patting the baby's back. He recalls a few strong images of the early days of his marriage. Ellie, hugely pregnant, sitting in the white bentwood rocker, a pot of geraniums flowering on the windowsill behind her. His newborn child, her face pink, her tiny hands balled up in tiny fists. Then Georgia appears, removing Lorenzo, thanking Walter, settling herself behind the counter again. There is a sudden cool place on Walter where the baby was.

"Do you have kids?" Georgia asks, arranging the shawl.

"My daughter is nineteen," says Walter. "She's a sophomore in college." He doesn't know what to say after that. "I love her very much," he adds, shyly.

"She must be proud of her old man."

"What?" Walter blushes. His finger has been touching the spine of his own book. One copy today.

"That's who you are, isn't it? *Millions of Picnics*? I recognized you the first time you came in. You look like Ronald Colman. I liked your book."

Walter nods. "Well, thank you. It happened pretty late in life so I'm a bit stunned."

"Late in life? Are you kidding? I'm forty-two with a

child. Don't talk to me about late in life. Late at night, now that's something else. Two A.M.? God." She nuzzles Lorenzo's little face.

"I'm up a good part of the night," says Walter, before he knows what he is saying. "I see well in the dark." This is what happens when he talks. He quickly turns his attention to a book on the table in front of him. As he opens it, he backs slowly away, so as to become invisible.

"You looking for anything special?" she asks, startling him.

"Who, me?" Walter wheels around guiltily.

"You. Is there anything I can help with? Anything particular you want?"

"Well, no, actually, I'm just browsing," he says uncomfortably. "Having a bookstore in the neighborhood is such a pleasure," he adds, lest she think him rude. Is there anything he wants? He wants his wife back.

"This has to be the ultimate in pleasure," she says, "the ultimate. Forget all else." And she gazes down at her baby boy, whose head below the curve of her breast is like a small moon rising behind the planet Milk.

THE FIRST NIGHT Ellie was gone Walter had thought he might not manage. He had spent two days in a hotel so as not to be around while Ellie packed. It was her suggestion, he had offered to help. But she had been right—it was hard for her to hide her excitement. When he got home he was tired, and part of him hoped against hope that he would open the door and find Ellie in the kitchen, pots of things simmering on the stove. "I changed my mind," he hoped to hear her say. "I must have been crazy." But instead he came into a quiet apartment. When he looked around at first everything seemed the same. She hadn't taken anything off the tables. A few books were missing and one rose-colored chair from the window. He went into the bathroom. Her toothbrush was gone and her shampoo. She'd left behind her dusty box of cotton balls. In the bedroom her bureau was bare and her closet empty. He had sat down on the edge of the bed and put his head in his hands. But then he had pulled himself together and poured himself a scotch. Looking for ice he saw she had bought him milk and orange juice and a new box of cereal. He sat at the table with his drink and looked around. It seemed impossible that he would have to live like this. Time was thickening all around him. He couldn't imagine getting through a single night this way, let alone the rest of his life. He dialed the number she had left pinned to his pillow but hung up after the first ring.

"Did you just call?" Ellie rang him back two seconds later.

"I didn't mean to," said Walter.

"I knew it was you. Go to sleep. Try and get some sleep." And she had hung up.

He hadn't slept that night, at least not that he'd noticed, but he had gotten up early and looked out the windows the next morning and the Mexicans had been on the roof of the hotel, singing. It was the first time he'd seen them and Walter had nearly wept with gratitude. "Look at that," he'd whispered. "They're making music."

Some weeks later he had pointed them out to Julie. "They're drinking, Dad," she'd said, looking briefly out the window. "In half an hour they'll be throwing each other off the roof."

AT NOON WALTER is on a bench on the median at Eightieth and Broadway. He has a bunch of daisies from Hector's (Walter never fails to bring flowers to his mother), a warm bagel in a paper bag on his lap, and a cup of coffee. Walter takes a bite of bagel, a swallow of sugary coffee. "You're a stick-in-the mud," Ellie had said to him, not always with humor in her voice. The fact is, Ellie wanted a change. He understands that now. Perhaps his rut had gone so deep he could no longer see over the sides.

At twelve-thirty Walter is opening the door to his mother's apartment, calling out as he enters, "Hello, Mom, Mrs. Tristen," and he walks into the living room, where his mother is already sitting in her wheelchair. (He could walk here in the dark too.) Walter's mother is dressed in a black blouse and a pair of black silk trousers. Her hands rest gracefully on her knees and on her head she wears an old-fashioned straw hat, a boater, he thinks she used to call it. Mrs. Tristen gets up from the green chair that had once upon a time belonged to Walter's father. "Mother is having a quiet day," she says, taking the flowers from him. There are more and more days when the old lady refuses to speak. It is as if a wire has gone down. He pictures such a wire, and the birds on it, and the birds taking flight somewhere inside her head as the wire goes down.

Walter thinks he could spend whole days without speaking too.

"Hello, Mom," he says anyway, reflex action, "hello, Mom," and he bends down and takes one of her hands, warm and papery in his. She turns her face away but covers his hand with her other one. "I think we will go out for an ice cream this afternoon," he says. "I think we have time before it rains, don't you, Mrs. Tristen?" He looks around the living room, the chintz chairs, the rose-colored rug, the filmy white curtains. He knows this room so well, the lamps, the small delicate tables with legs like fawns. Nothing has changed in fifty years. His father's seersucker bathrobe still hangs on the back of the bathroom door.

"Mother," he says, "we will go for our walk now. Are you quite ready?"

As he pushes the wheelchair toward Broadway the sun

shines. Walter is wearing a short-sleeved shirt. His mother would have criticized this a few years ago. "A gentleman does not wear short sleeves on the street," she would say, frowning, or, "A gentleman never wears brown." He looks down at the top of his mother's straw hat. Something about the way she sits so properly in the wheelchair moves him terribly and his eyes and nose prick with tears. He stops at the corner of Columbus and Eighty-sixth and reaches down to pat her shoulder. "It's a beautiful day, Mother. We're out on a beautiful day."

Walter stops at the Häagen-Dazs ice cream store and buys his mother a single scoop of vanilla in a cup. He sits himself down on the bench outside, drawing his mother's wheelchair up close so that their knees are nearly touching. Slowly she eats. He holds her paper cup and places the napkin in her right hand. She opens her mouth and Walter carefully, delicately deposits a spoonful inside, and then she closes her mouth. She doesn't move her jaws. She doesn't change her expression. A full minute goes by and then she opens her mouth again. There is a serenity about her these days, and her face is beautiful, softer. As a mother she was rather remote, she was solemn and upright, she had dignity and taste, she read history and played the piano. She never liked Ellie, not from the very first. "She won't do for you, Walter," his mother had said. "She is not one of us and she won't have your best interests in mind. Mark my words." Walter wonders if his mother had been right after all, right, but for all the wrong reasons. "I love her," he had said, "and she loves me." They had been sitting at the breakfast table, his mother buttering toast. "Piffle," his mother had replied. "Love is a detail, Walter. There's a lot of life to get through and love is only part of it. A detail. A scrap of ribbon."

Walter leans forward. He has been gazing into space, the ice cream melting on the silver spoon he always brings along, carefully wrapping it in a napkin for the trip home in his pocket. Mother always despised the taste of plastic. It will be her birthday soon. "My mother sails into her ninety-sixth year," he thinks, "a sleeping ship." Her skin is whiter than flour, her eyes enormous, milky now, and he is not certain what she is seeing when she looks at him. But today she suddenly says in her old cracked teacup of a voice, "I love you," with such a fervor that it brings tears to Walter's eyes. "I love you too, Mother," he says, and pats her hand where it rests on the arm of the chair and she seizes his with the uncanny strength she sometimes still displays, pressing his hand to her cheek. "I love you," she says again.

"I love you too," he repeats, eyes brimming. Grateful to whatever it is that allowed him to love her at long last.

• • •

HE: *Forgive me if I continue to bother you with questions. I'd like to get back to needs and purposes. What possible needs could you have, what possible purposes?*

IT: *Let me tell you about needs first. Since we have no material ones and no religious beliefs, our needs are all self-created and might be called in your terms intellectual and emotional. The main thing, the thing that provides most of our drive, is curiosity. Although we know everything in general, the world is much too complex to be known in any sort of detail. It's of such unimaginable richness that it would take an infinite Being to know it all. So we are always being surprised, often very surprised, at what we find in our explorations and in each other. We want to be surprised, and need to be. Further than that—and doubtless due to our animal origins—we are social Beings and need to be with other Entities. Without each other it would be an intolerably dull universe.*

WALTER LOOKS AT his watch. Ellie expects him at five. He decides it wouldn't hurt to shave again. He puts on his pale blue shirt (a birthday present from Julie last year, worn once) and the bow tie (a birthday present from Ellie four years ago, worn never). When he goes into the subway the fact that the train has just pulled in he takes as a good omen.

Ellie's small apartment is a third-floor walk-up. He

rings the downstairs buzzer now, and when she buzzes him in he climbs the wooden staircase, which smells musty and makes him feel young again. He is ready for anything, he thinks. He is ready to receive his wife back into his life, with bells on. That is what he has planned to say. "Would you like me to come home?" he has imagined Ellie asking. "With bells on," he has declared in his mind.

Ellie answers the door with a distracted air, her hair in disarray. She is wearing an old sweater over a pair of jeans. Her feet are bare. He bends to kiss her but she avoids his mouth. "I'm smoking again," she explains. "You won't approve." He feels instantly uncomfortable in his bow tie.

"Come in, come in," she says. "Don't mind the mess."

"What's happening down here?" he asks. There are boxes everywhere, stacked against the wall. The bookcases are empty. He looks at her. "Ellie?"

"Walter. Oh Walter," says Ellie, and she sinks down onto the blue couch. "Christ. I don't know how to tell you."

"Is everything all right?" he asks, sitting next to her. "Are you ill? Is Julie all right? What's wrong? Ellie, tell me!" He is suddenly terrified. His heart is beating quickly and he feels light-headed. Something in her face is frightening him.

Her voice is unfamiliar because it is shaky. "Walter. I'm moving."

"That's not funny. You're kidding, aren't you?" He pats her hand, smiling and looking at her, but she shakes her head.

"I knew this would be hard. Walter, I'm moving to Brooklyn. I may be getting married again."

"You're what?"

"Oh, Walt." And Ellie begins to cry. Shaken, Walter reaches for the handkerchief in his pocket and hands it to his former wife, his old friend.

"Ellie. This is such a surprise. Are you certain? Just the other night I thought—"

"I know, I know. I wanted to tell you then but I couldn't." Her face is blotchy and her eyes turn red at the rims and her mouth quivers. "I just couldn't." He doesn't know what to say so he hugs her and she trembles in his arms. "I never meant this," she says. "I didn't plan this to happen."

"But are you quite sure? I mean, Ellie, have you thought this through? Who is it? I thought you wanted to be alone," he says.

"So did I."

The surface of Walter, his skin, seems to be registering the exact temperature of the air, which is warm, but underneath he has turned cold.

"He's nice," Ellie is snuffling and saying. "He likes your book."

"I'm gratified to hear it," says Walter. Really, it is amazing, *he turned cold* is exactly right. There must be some evolutionary advantage.

"Walter, you're my oldest friend. Try to be happy for me."

"And you're mine, Ellie. Are you really doing this?"

"I don't know," she says. "I think so."

"I don't want you to." Even now help must be bobsledding to whatever part of Walter most needs it.

"It might be a disaster. It probably will be a disaster," she says.

"I would like that. I don't want you to go." Walter repeats himself, looking at her urgently. "Does Julie know?"

Ellie nods.

"And?"

"She is worried about you."

"Have you given any thought to our, you know, joining forces again?"

At first Ellie doesn't speak. "We're friends, Walt. That's what we are. We're friends."

He picks up his jacket from the back of the chair.

"Where are you going?" she says, getting up.

"I am going to go home now and try to absorb all this news."

"Walter?" he hears her calling down the stairs after him but he is gone.

WALTER IS STANDING outside the bookstore again. His bow tie is in his pocket. Georgia is still there; her right hand rocks the little chair where Lorenzo sleeps, the other twirls her hair as she reads. There are no customers. He can't go in, how can he possibly go in? After all, what would he say? Could I hold your child a moment? He wants to remember Ellie with the geraniums behind her again. Where did all that go? Not nowhere, it doesn't just disappear, does it? If he closes his eyes he can have it all back again, however briefly, the curtains blowing a little, everything still to come.

Inside the store Georgia stretches and looks at her watch. Walter steps away from the window. Another image comes. A row of his black socks, skinny as cigars, hanging over the shower rod. The first time he'd filled the sink with soapy water he'd been astonished by how insubstantial a man's sock got when it was wet.

Walking home, Walter waits for the light on Broadway and 108th. A fire engine comes screaming by and a middle-aged woman standing next to him jumps. When the truck has passed she shakes her head and says, "Edith. Get ahold of yourself."

"Walter," thinks Walter, "get ahold of yourself." The woman named Edith walks out against the light. She is wearing a black hat with—what? cherries?—on the brim.

WALTER IS SITTING in Julie's room, a cigarette in one hand. In his life Walter has smoked parts of six cigarettes, and this is his seventh. He coughs horribly. How can anyone do this, he wants to know. On his lap is a shoebox full of snapshots. Julie at four, speaking to the waves on a beach, in her red, white, and blue bathing suit, her hair curly and tousled by wind. A close-up of the bottom of Walter's left foot, lying on a beach towel, taken probably by his daughter. Ellie hunched over a Thanksgiving turkey, his own mother and father, looking impossibly young, sitting on either side of her, Julie in his mother's arms. Strange sounds are coming from Walter.

"Dad! What are you doing in here?" Julie is standing in the doorway but he is afraid to look at her because he is so weepy. How did he not hear her come in?

"Catching my breath," he says, the first thing that comes to mind.

"So she told you, huh. I told her she had to. It wasn't fair." Julie comes into the room and sits down on the bed. "It sucks, doesn't it, Dad."

"No, not at all, not at all. This is a good thing for your mother. I take my hat off to her, in fact. A new life. How are you taking the news? Are you all right? You know you always have a home here with me."

"I know that, Dad. I wasn't worried."

"I'm absolutely fine, by the way. Really fine." He smiles and reaches over to pat her knee.

Julie takes a deep breath. "So you're not going to be lonely? You're not mad at Mom?" There is such relief on her face. Walter hesitates.

"Did I tell you I have a date?"

"Get out! You do? Why didn't you tell me? Who is it?"

"A very nice woman in the publishing business. I remind her of Ronald Colman. We've become friends in recent weeks. I am taking her out to dinner next week." As he speaks Walter realizes such a thing is actually possible.

HE: *And what about Purpose? Don't just say that it's not possible to explain it to me. You are a Superior Being, you know me inside and out, surely you can find a way of conveying at least the possibility of a Purpose.*

IT: *Well, I'll try. Perhaps it's easier to start with what our purposes are not. They certainly don't include maximizing things like power or pleasure or even "happiness." We try to go on existing, though none of us in our right minds thinks that there is any intrinsic meaning to our lives. (By the way, there are those of us that are not in our right minds.) The creators of our particular entities were very aware of the problems of purpose, having suffered from it themselves for untold ages. So they did two things: they amplified to an extreme degree the animal striving for survival and they added a new*

instinct of comparable force. The closest thing in your experi-
ence to the new instinct is the sense of beauty. These new sen-
sibilities, extraordinarily diversified and strongly reinforced
by the already powerful curiosity of our species, provide a
motivation which almost never fails for most of us. Those for
whom it does fail do exist, and often they go mad or turn
themselves off. These sensibilities enable us to create works of
"Art" that are extraordinary even by our own standards.
They may be material objects, mathematical ideas, even lit-
erature of a kind. And that is the basis for our social life; we
trade these things among ourselves, communicate with each
other about them, in some way even judge them.

HE: I don't find that so hard to comprehend, but I'd hoped
for a little more satisfying solution.

AT THREE WALTER is up again, eating his cornflakes. He
walks around the apartment in the dark, his bowl of cornflakes in one hand, his spoon in the other. Julie is asleep,
he has already looked in on her. Under his bare feet he
feels the floor go from wood to the worn red rug and back
again. The linoleum of the kitchen is smooth and cool. He
makes his rounds in the dark, touching things. He stops
to take a handkerchief from his bathrobe and blow his
nose. Out the kitchen window on the fourth floor across
the street the light is on as always. He has checked. A
plant light maybe. What if it is? Plants are beautiful. He

thinks of his mother's African violets growing out of their pots. He thinks of geraniums.

The light is on now in Walter's bedroom. He sits at the chair by the window, his feet on the radiator cover as he writes, and chews his pen and writes some more. He looks up from the page. The sky above the city is that violet purple he loves. The red beacon is blinking on and off in the distance. The rest of the city is dark. Perhaps someone will see his light and take heart. He hopes so.

At dawn Walter stretches and rubs his eyes. He stands and looks down from the window again. There on the roof he sees a man and boy emerge from the blue door. Father and son? Walter thinks so. They carry a big sack between them and a long cylinder of what turns out to be brown wrapping paper which they unroll on the roof, kneeling down, weighing the corners with bricks. Next they reach into the sack, withdrawing small misshapen red things. Walter squints to see better. Boiled lobsters? Ridiculous. Crabs? Now the man looks up at the sky, which is cloudless and already warmer than yesterday. The boy spreads more of the strange red things on the paper. Walter squints. Red peppers. Of course! They are drying red chili peppers on the roof across the street.

As Walter begins to smile another man appears, with a guitar. Walter begins to strum the air, humming to himself, moving this way and that in front of the window.

EDITH'S WARDROBE

HATS

EDITH DIDN'T REALLY know which hat. There were a whole bunch of them on the little stand and she took down a blue felt with a red rose on the brim. She turned it over to see where the label was so she could tell back from front, although maybe there was no such thing anymore as back and front. She placed the hat carefully on top of her head, the label in the back (the rose off center), and then she gently pulled it down her forehead. The hat felt snug around her head, tight and oddly reassuring. It made Edith think about her skull, and the delicate brain inside, and how nicely everything worked. She looked at her reflection in the mirror that sat at a tilt on the counter, and automatically she made her mirror face, lips pursed, eyes slightly narrowed. It was a forties face, a femme fatale face, and Edith had been making it since she was twelve years old.

"May I?" asked the pretty Chinese salesgirl behind the counter, and without waiting for Edith to answer she reached across and with cool sure hands she tugged the hat down over Edith's left ear, leaving the other naked and, Edith felt, unecessarily exposed. "Looks good at an angle," said the young woman, and she smiled at Edith and motioned to the mirror. Edith blushed. "Oh," she said, "thank you." She looked in the mirror again just to be polite and then she quickly pulled the hat off and patted her hair. "Not really for me," she said apologetically, and replaced the hat on its little sponge rubber pad. "Thank you, though."

The girl continued to smile and Edith pulled down a different hat, an enormous greenish beret-looking affair, and Edith put it back without trying it on. It looked awfully saggy and Edith thought it would droop down the back of her coat like some hideous net. Edith was wearing her good gray coat, the warm one she had gotten last year on sale. It wasn't a frumpy coat—Edith wasn't a frump, it was a middle-aged coat for a middle-aged person. You could not distinguish two separate breasts beneath it, just a broad dignified expanse that sloped more or less outward and dropped off more or less downward over the substantial person that Edith had, over the years, become. Her only ornament was a silver sea turtle, which clambered ever up toward Edith's shoulder.

Edith reached now for a dark blue hat but the salesgirl handed her instead a floppy black bonnet with red and yellow cherries in a big bunch at the front, if that was the front, the whole thing a bit shapeless and haphazard looking. Edith remembered sucking on some ornamental cherries once when she was small, not giving up at the pasty, disappointing taste. She remembered her mother taking them out of her mouth, fussing and scolding as she did so. This was perhaps Edith's earliest memory.

Edith stood still now as the girl positioned the hat on her head. There was a wire at the outermost part of the brim which reminded Edith of a run-over lampshade, but she didn't say so. The girl's fingers brushing Edith's cheek made Edith feel suddenly sleepy and she said, "Is this a warm hat?" instead of "Do I look silly?," not wanting to look in the mirror but doing so anyway. Actually, the hat looked rather nice on her and the cherries gave her coat a little lift. But it was completely out of the question and she took it off carefully and handed it back to the girl. "I don't know," said Edith.

"Looked very nice," said the girl. "One of a kind." She smiled at Edith, revealing extremely white teeth.

Edith reached again for the small blue hat. It was really more of a knitted cap, the kind sailors wore. "I knew somebody had a hat like this once," said Edith, looking in the mirror as she raised her eyebrows and lowered the cap over her head. The girl leaned forward and began to tuck stray strands of Edith's hair under the cap but Edith drew back as politely as she could. "You probably weren't even born then," said Edith, and she smiled her own nicest smile. The girl nodded and Edith thought how pretty she was, beautiful almost. "He saw me in my nightgown once," Edith continued, lowering her voice. "Of course, that's nothing in today's world, but in 1953, I can tell you, it was considered very risqué." The girl disappeared down behind the counter and Edith heard the rustling of tissue paper and then the girl stood up again. "I walked in my sleep, you see," said Edith. "I was standing on our front lawn in my white nightgown and a pair of red rubber boots, if you can believe such a thing. It was raining." Edith looked at the girl to see if she could believe such a thing but couldn't read her expression. "He took my upper arm, you see, very gently, so as not to wake me"— Edith illustrated by grabbing the upper part of her right arm with her left hand—"only I must have been awake already because I can recall everything."

"Really." The girl neatened up a pile of pink tissue paper.

"Yes, indeed. He led me back inside the house and I could smell his breath because he had been drinking. He had a cigarette in his mouth the entire time, I remember distinctly, although it had gone out in the rain. He put his cap on my head which was silly because it was as wet as my hair and he sat me down on a kitchen chair. Then he said, 'See you later, Edith,' and he left." Edith noticed the girl had sunk to her knees again behind the counter and all she could see was the top of her head. Edith was forced to raise her voice. "You know, he went to prison several months later for burglary. My mother knew his parents.

We didn't see them for the longest time." Edith fell silent. "I wasn't a popular girl. But I always had a very small waist."

The girl had several boxes on top of the counter and she was laying tissue paper in them now. "Would you like to see something else?" Her smile was friendly.

"Of course, I believed myself to be in love with him for a week after, maybe a month." Edith looked at herself again in the mirror. "Do you think this hat makes my head look too small?"

"Excuse me?" the girl answered.

"Does it look as if I've got a little head?"

"No," said the girl. "No, not at all. It looks fine. Very nice."

"Because that's the one thing you can't change," said Edith. "A little head. There's nothing you can do about it. I have a horror of appearing to have a little head," said Edith, and she took a small mirror out of her bag. Edith looked at herself from the side, from all angles. "I was too shy to speak to him again. My mother made me return the hat. I'm afraid I may have snubbed him." Edith satisfied herself that her head appeared to be a normal size. "I think I'll take the other one. Please. After all. The one with the cherries."

Edith wore her new hat out of the store. On the street,

she caught sight of herself in a shop window and she took it off and carried it in her hand. A block later she put it back on; then, crossing Broadway against the light, she took it off again. And so it continued, all the way home.

NEGLIGEE

"NEGLIGEE," SAID EDITH, forcing the word with some difficulty from her mouth.

"For madam?"

"For someone about my size," said Edith humbly. "My friend is too sick to shop."

Murmurs of sympathy.

"Well, not sick, exactly. She broke her leg," said Edith. "Well, actually, just one of the small bones in her foot," Edith went on, warming to it. "A can of soup fell on it. Unopened. A big can. The red looks nice. No, the black looks nice. She'll like the little roses, I think. Her husband is coming back from a long trip," Edith found it necessary to add. "Is there a bottom part too?"

Edith paid for the tiny thing, assured by the saleslady that this would be flattering to the full-figured woman.

Edith took the plane to Richmond. "I am taking a flier on love," whispered Edith on the plane, sitting by the window, ripping open the bags of peanuts. She watched the houses shrink, the ribbons of road start to stretch out and uncurl beneath her. She wondered what would happen to the plane if she stopped concentrating. "If he's there, he's there," thought Edith philosophically.

He was there but he didn't recognize Edith's voice. "Who is this?" he said.

"Don't you remember?" said Edith. She had packed nothing but the tiny nightie. She had left her return ticket open. It smelled good in Richmond. She loved the smell of rotting vegetation. "Don't you remember?" said Edith. "We had three margaritas? After your talk? You said to call if I was ever in Richmond and now here I am." Edith remembered everything. She had stood pink and perspiring in his hotel room wearing her big snowsuit and her scarf and he had worn his gray parka with the stain on the pocket and he had kissed her seven times. She remembered everything although she had been a bit tipsy.

"Tippecanoe and Tyler too," she had chortled all the way home in the taxi. His name was Tyler, and he was a travel writer, and she had sat next to him in Mrs. Keosian's ninth-grade science class. Her mother had known his mother. Edith had read everything he had ever written. Edith had gone to a lecture he gave which was so ill-attended that she had had no trouble speaking to him after it was over. They had been the only two people in the auditorium. She had offered herself as a companion for coffee, and he had hesitated and then accepted. He had taken her elbow, and guided her across the streets. They had not gone out for coffee, he had taken her to Brat's and ordered margaritas for her, a double scotch on the rocks for himself. "So," he had said when they were sitting at a dark scarred little table in the back, "where have you run across my work?" Later, in his hotel room, Edith had never even taken off her coat. After several minutes of kissing he had pushed her away and regarded her at arm's length. "Ah, Edith," he had said, perspiring a bit himself. "Well. It's getting quite late and I have to catch a very early plane. Let me find you a cab. No, I insist." Edith's mouth was still hot from kissing. She stood before him, a trembly maiden of fifty-two. "You can call me, Edith, if you ever come to Richmond," Tyler had said kindly as he shook her hand. He had given the driver a twenty and told him to keep the change. It was so generous of him, Edith had thought, tipsy and happy and bewildered by love.

"YOU'RE WHERE?" TYLER sounded alarmed. "Where are you staying, Edith?"

"With you," said Edith, feeling warm. Her stockings were too hot for this weather. She put her little bag on the floor between her feet and unbuttoned her big coat. It was very, very warm here. "I've come down for the weekend." Edith tried to sound casual.

"My god," he said, and there was a long pause. Edith waited, her left foot rubbing her right ankle where something must have bitten her already. "All right, Edith," he said finally, but his voice sounded so grim.

Tyler picked her up in the reddest car Edith ever had seen. "My," she said, settling herself in the front seat with a happy fuss. "This is the just the reddest car. It's so interesting here." Edith looked out of the window, which she had rolled all the way down. Tyler asked her to roll it back up again. He had air-conditioning in his car. Everyone had air-conditioning everywhere down South.

"I'M AFRAID, EDITH," said Tyler when they had gotten under way, "I'm afraid"—he shook his head sorrowfully— "you've come at a bad time for me. If you'd care to stay in my guest room I would be happy to have you. Otherwise—" He broke off. He cleared his throat. Edith studied a small red bump on the back of her left hand. She brought it close to her face for a better look. She wondered what chiggers looked like, actually. "My psychiatrist has warned me against starting, you know, a new relationship right now. We've reached a turning point in my analysis, and she feels it would be destructive for me to engage in anything intimate with a new woman at the moment, no matter how"—he smiled at Edith—"appealing she might be. I'm sure you understand what I'm talking about." And Tyler studied the road ahead, where a car was pulling into his lane.

Edith, blushing furiously, understood. "Oh," she said, "I don't mind. I'm just down for the day anyway. I always do this. I like to have a look at other parts of the United States whenever I get a chance. And mother was having company today so I thought to myself, what a good time to visit Richmond. So historical." Edith's voice grew husky. She too cleared her throat. She began scratching the back of her hand. She hoped he would have calamine lotion in his house, but she wasn't going to ask him.

Tyler's walls were lined with books and his sliding kitchen doors were made of glass. He had a small garden and a hanging jasmine plant. Edith stood beneath it while he was out. She breathed in the sweet sweet smell. "We could be so happy here," she whispered. Tyler had many appointments, and Edith had not given him any warning. He was sorry, but this was a normal day of work for him and he hoped she would be all right alone. "You won't be too bored, I hope," he said. "Oh, no," said Edith. "There is so much to read here." And she smiled at him as he left, wanting to wave from the front door. She stood there with her hand up but he didn't turn around. He just got into his car and drove away. "After all," said Edith to herself, "I'm not his wife." Edith sat down at the kitchen table with a book by Tyler Fletcher in her lap. She studied photographs of him trekking up mountainsides, picking his way across bogs. She studied the muscles in his calves. The phone rang and rang but Tyler had said the machine would pick up any calls. She should not bother herself.

Tyler had showed her how to turn down the sound if it got too troublesome. The blinking red light was for messages. Soon it was blinking so fast Edith couldn't count the calls. The phone rang fifty times. The sound was turned off on the answering machine, so Edith couldn't hear any of the messages. Edith didn't dare go upstairs. Suppose he came home unexpectedly and found her there, snooping?

Edith made herself a cup of coffee. He had a drip coffeepot but his coffee had that horrible almond flavor and Edith had to pour it down the sink. At three-thirty, Edith ventured outside for a brief walk. But really, his was just a street like other streets, and she was afraid people would wonder who she was and what she was doing there. Along the way she sustained several other small bites. She came back after only five minutes and she looked in his medicine chest. No calamine. Only aftershave. Six different kinds of aftershave. She picked her favorite, which was what she thought he had smelled like the night he had kissed her so many times. Edith put the bottle in her pocket. "No," she said, shaking her head. "Absolutely not." And she put it back on the shelf. His medicine chest was clean and orderly. She looked inside his laundry hamper. The clothes in there were folded too. Men's blue boxer shorts. She wanted to pick up a pair but she couldn't bring herself to do that. She thought again of his kisses and the memory caused little shocks on the palms of her hands, the soles of her feet. "How odd," she thought. "It really is electricity."

When Tyler got home, he put a bag of groceries on the counter. The phone rang and he spoke into it with a low voice. "Tomorrow," she heard him say. "Yes. I promise." Edith felt so silly. She wanted to disappear. But she was much too big to disappear. She decided to make the best of it. She cooked an omelet. Edith was good with eggs and butter, and her omelets were always tender and brown. "This is a symphony," said Tyler, taking a bite, "a poem and a symphony."

"This is my specialty," said Edith, proud and happy. "One of my specialties." And she ate her omelet with a big spoon.

They watched trout fishing on late-night TV. Large-mouth-bass fishing, taught by the Bass Master. It was for some reason terribly funny. They both laughed hysterically. Edith found herself wanting to sit closer and closer, but Tyler had put a pillow between them to rest his arm. Tears came to their eyes. Edith's stomach began to hurt and she had to cry out. "No," she said. "Stop. Don't. It's too funny!" she shouted, doubling over like a big piece of bread.

"I never laugh this hard," said Tyler with a puzzled expression on his face and Edith thought he might be going to kiss her. "Good night," he said instead. On Edith's bed-side table was a book called *A Man Called Peter*. Also a copy of *Spartacus*. Edith took this as a joke and she read the first lines of both books. Then she put them back care-fully. The bed was small, a cot really. She turned on the air conditioner, then turned it off again. She opened her overnight bag and took out the negligee. It took her some time to figure out how it went, because it had no regular arms or legs, and then when she got it on she wanted to see how it looked, but there was no mirror in the bed-room except a tiny one above the bureau in which Edith could see no more than her face. Edith tiptoed down the hall to the bathroom and climbed up on the edge of the tub to look in the mirror. She turned this way and that. "Well," she said, "it's not too bad, really." On her way back to bed she looked up the long stairs to Tyler's room. He had already turned out his lights. It was completely dark up there. What would happen if she just went up and lay down in the bed next to him? It wouldn't be good man-ners, certainly. And she might be sent back downstairs again and that would be the most embarrassing thing that had ever happened to Edith, worse than anything. So Edith climbed into the little bed and she slept the night in her negligee, which itched her, and by morning, what with scratching and adjusting and flailing about in a strange bed, the thing had torn and Edith found it in the bed underneath her. It had come right off in the night. Perhaps it had not been well made, perhaps they were not meant for actual sleeping. Edith packed it anyway; she was afraid Tyler would find it if she threw it away. Besides, it was a souvenir of sorts.

In the morning Tyler was in a hurry. He needed to get to a big meeting that day and he was anxious to drive Edith to the airport. On top of that, his phone was ringing again. "It was awfully good of you to come," said Tyler to Edith, holding open the front door. The telephone rang again. Tyler spoke less softly this time. "Yes," he said, "I realize that," and he put the phone down hard. Edith was sure they would never have spoken to each other like that. Tyler was warming up the engine and Edith took a last look around. "Good-bye house," she said, holding a breath of jasmine all the way to the car.

Before they drove away, Edith ran back inside. She thought she might have forgotten something on the night table. On the way out, she dropped a teacup into Tyler's disposal, pushing it well down. It would be difficult to retrieve. This gave her some satisfaction, and she smiled. She just wanted to break something of his, she didn't know why.

GLOVES

EDITH'S MOTHER WAS in and out of the hospital all spring. Fluids dripped into her arm, the oxygen tank made a gurgling that sounded like surf. "Where are we?" Edith's mother asked often. "We're in New York City," said Edith. "You're in the hospital."

"What's that noise?" Edith's mother sounded suspicious.

"What noise?" Edith strained to hear.

"That noise. That ocean noise."

"I think that's the oxygen, Mother," said Edith.

"What's out there then?" asked Edith's mother, pointing to the window.

Edith got up from her chair and looked through a slat of the venetian blind. "More hospital," she answered truthfully, "and some river."

"Thank god," said Edith's mother. "I thought we were in Hawaii."

Home again, the nurses who cared for Edith's mother wore rubber gloves for certain procedures. There was no word to describe the sound these gloves made going on or coming off. It was a sound unlike any other. Brisk, you could say, thought Edith. Brisk. These were good women and efficient and there was nothing for Edith to do. Still, her mother liked Edith's presence in the room, and always knew when Edith got up to leave. "Where are you going, Edith," she said sharply, even when her eyes were closed. It was Edith's knees creaking. Or the air she displaced, creating a draft.

"Nowhere, mother," said Edith.

"I could use a glass of something cold," said her mother. "Tea might be nice." But she was asleep when Edith brought it back. "You forgot the ice," said her mother later when she woke. But she was joking.

Edith's mother beckoned Edith to come close. Edith drew her chair up next to the bed and leaned over. "Watch those girls," said her mother in a loud whisper. "See that they don't steal anything else." Edith's mother had been imagining things missing. A pillow. An extension cord. An old watchband gone from the windowsill. "Mother," said Edith. "Everything is where it is supposed to be."

"I know what I know," said her mother and set her lips in a maddening smile. Edith's mother's hair was going white.

"Don't go through my things," said Edith's mother. "I'm not dead yet, you know." Edith had quietly opened the top drawer of her mother's bureau.

"I am getting you a handkerchief," said Edith, but she was slipping a pair of gloves into the pocket of her dress.

"They won't fit you, Edith," said her mother. "I have small hands."

Edith's pocket were crammed. Lipsticks, a pair of man-icure scissors, coins from the top of her mother's dresser. This was not stealing. It would bring her mother luck, she thought. She was going to give everything back. When she examined it all later in her own room, her heart pounding like a thief, Edith saw the gloves were her fa-vorite kind, kid gloves that smelled so sweet. She held them up to her face and breathed in the sweet smell. She opened a different drawer the next day. "Edith," said her mother. "Come away from there." Edith did as she was told, although she was almost fifty-three years old. She sat down in the chair by her mother's bed. Edith fingered the pearls in her pocket. Her mother had always worn these pearls. She had taught Edith to test a pearl between her teeth. She had told Edith they would be hers someday. Someday was not so interesting. Edith didn't want them someday. Everything seemed so much more valuable while her mother was alive. She didn't want pearls. She wanted her mother's pearls while her mother was still alive. Later, she put them back. The jewelry box had a squeaky lid but her mother did not seem to mind this time.

"Don't come too close," whispered her mother, pushing Edith away. "I don't want you catching anything." Edith's mother's breathing reminded Edith of footsteps, slow and deliberate with long pauses between, because of the dark, because of the unfamiliarity of the terrain.

Edith's mother died in her sleep. Edith was asleep too. The nurse shook Edith's shoulder and Edith woke instantly. The nurse left Edith alone with her mother's body. Edith looked from her mother's face to the ceiling. She waved at the ceiling because she had read that the dying person looks down at the bed. "Good-bye, Mother," Edith said to the ceiling. She held her mother's hand. She kissed her mother's forehead. Edith didn't want to leave the room. She wasn't sure where to go. Surely everything had changed.

She put on her big flowered nightgown and lay down on the couch. She couldn't go to sleep and she couldn't stay awake. She wasn't sure what to do with herself so she got up and ran water for a bath. She poured in soap flakes and swirled up the suds. She took off her nightgown and climbed in, gingerly lowering her large white body into the tub. What a lot of Edith there seemed to be. She lay back. She lifted one leg out of the water, then the other. Here I am, thought Edith. She made gloves out of the soapsuds, short churchy ones that covered only her hands, then long creamy white evening gloves that extended to her elbows and above, reaching almost to her armpits.

HANDKERCHIEFS

EDITH DID NOT cry. Her mother had had a rich and interesting life and at the end she had wished for death. During the final week Edith's mother had called out "I love you, I love you," to an unseen presence in the room. Perhaps Edith's father, come back as a ghost to help his wife into the next world. Edith tried to keep her face calm at these moments, lest her father's ghost think less of her. He had been a handsome man, Edith an awkward child.

Her mother had never cried either, if the abundance of unused handkerchiefs in her bottom drawer meant anything. Her mother had never cried, nor had she been sick a day in her life until what took her away at the end. Edith sat on the floor next to the dresser, looking at these handkerchiefs, many in their original cellophane envelopes. "I bought this for her," said Edith. The hankie in question was linen, in the corner a large purple petunia. Something about the color made Edith homesick, but she knew not for what since she was home, had always been home. She slid the handkerchief out of its wrapper and into her pocket. She was going out this morning, despite the risk of running into Mr. Feeley, and she wanted something to blot her eyes with if the pollen was flying. Her eyes had been bothering her lately, quite red in the mornings.

Edith's knees creaked as she got to her feet, although she was still every bit as strong as she ever had been.

Edith was almost ashamed of her own loss next to that of Mr. Feeley. What a shabby grief was hers when you considered the poor old widower. Just as Edith would be thinking about her mother she would remember Mrs. Feeley, and the love the two Feeleys had had for each other, and how they had been inseparable, husband and wife, married for sixty years, and she felt ashamed at her own sorry state. Mr. Feeley's suffering was so absolute as to strike poor Edith dumb. What could she possibly say in the face of such a loss? She sometimes stayed indoors for days on end just to avoid meeting Mr. Feeley, king of grief. She had lain under the bedclothes unwilling to show her face after she had heard the news. (Once Mrs. Feeley had sent a Jell-O salad to her mother. "Get that out of my house," Edith's mother had said, and Edith had swept the Jell-O into a bowl and returned the dish. Later she'd eaten the salad herself. "What became of that dreadful midwestern mess," Edith's mother had asked. "You didn't eat it, did you? Oh, *Edith*.")

But today she found no food in the kitchen and realized she had been indoors for four days without removing her nightgown. "Snap out of it," said Edith, "or you'll end up in the window dusting a fern." She cleaned up the many cups and saucers half full of milky tea and the copper bowl full of orange peels. She stacked the unread newspapers neatly on the extra kitchen chair. She bathed and dressed and left the apartment, checking in her bag for the keys three times before actually closing the door behind her.

EDITH WAS WALKING up toward Broadway, passing the Single Woman's Bookstore, when Mr. Feeley hove into view. She had nowhere to hide, not really, unless she ducked into the shop, and she could see through the window that Georgia, the proprietress, had one breast exposed for her baby boy and Edith just didn't feel up to that. So she took a deep breath and approached Mr. Feeley, holding out her hand.

"I am so very sorry," she said, offering her hand and trying to breathe through her mouth. His nails were unkempt, his hair wild, he smelled (could it be true?) of actual urine. Good Lord, thought Edith, real grief is so untidy.

"My wife died," said Mr. Feeley. "My Lois."

"Oh yes, I know, and I am so sorry."

"She died. She left me here by myself. She's gone, you know." His shoulders had begun to shake, and his left hand went toward his face, she saw his sleeve silvery with dried mucus. "I hung on for her, and see what happened. I'm alone now."

"Oh dear, Mr. Feeley," said Edith. There were crumbs on his chin. Saltines? He was wearing bedroom slippers.

"You know, I start to say something to her and then I see her chair is empty."

"I'm sure it must be very hard, Mr. Feeley." She patted his shoulder.

"Call me Martin. The worst is that I see her all the time now. That's how you know they're dead," he whispered, "when you start to see them in subways."

Edith, who just four days ago had been stabbed through the heart by a woman in a wheelchair who from the back looked like her mother, and had had to stifle the cry "Mother!" knew what Mr. Feeley meant. When she had caught up she had seen the woman was a much younger person, and had a cheerful face.

"How is your mother?" asked Mr Feeley suddenly.

"Well, that's the thing," Edith began but he interrupted her.

"Keeping fit, is she? You tell her I'll be dropping by," he said. "Your mother was one of the finest actresses of her generation." He was shaking his finger near Edith's face. "Mrs. Feeley loved her. We never missed a Harriet Tallmadge film. Never. You tell your mother that from me, will you? My Lois loved her work."

"She will be so gratified," said Edith, "to hear it."

"I'm ready to go myself, you know."

"Oh, Mr. Feeley," Edith began, not knowing what to say.

"It's true. Why not speak the truth. Mrs. Feeley was not afraid. She said she wasn't afraid. 'I've always liked to travel,' she said. I miss her," he said, bits of saltine-like crumbs flying into the air. Edith pictured God, a messy eater with crumbs in his beard, before he created the solar systems, napkins. He spoke out of loneliness, after a meal, and the flying crumbs and spittle became stars and planets. "A couple of pears would be nice," said Mr. Feeley. "Not too ripe, not too many dents and bruises. If it wouldn't be too much trouble."

"Yes, certainly," said Edith. "And I'll just ring your bell when I come back, shall I?"

"I may be resting," said Mr. Feeley. "Just hang it from the doorknob."

A few blocks down Broadway Edith took out her handkerchief. "I know just how old I was," she said, "six. And I thought this the prettiest thing I ever saw. And my mother saved it all these years. Imagine." She stood in front of the New Delhi Restaurant, which had closed soon after opening. Its tattered plastic flags blew cheerfully in the breeze, unaware that the festivities were over. Edith peered in the window. On a table stood a stack of white plates at the ready. They looked so eager, but had been abandoned. Inanimate objects were having too strong an effect on Edith. "I am a stack of white plates," said Edith to herself. On the way home she bought three pears but ate two of them herself on the street, one after the other, wiping her chin with the handkerchief.

FUR COAT

THE CRAZY LADY began to shout just as Edith's coffee arrived. "Oh dear," thought Edith, "Esmerelda." This was not, of course, the woman's name, but you couldn't just call someone the crazy lady, not forever, not even in your own mind, and Edith had settled on Esmerelda. Not that the woman looked like an Esmerelda; she was Chinese, or Tibetan, perhaps even an Eskimo, but she felt like an Esmerelda, at least to Edith, for whom the name conjured up somebody doomed by (among other things) love. Edith dropped the thin curl of lemon peel into her espresso and then turned sideways in her chair to look down the street. Poor Esmerelda, there she certainly was, gesturing at nobody Edith could see, and shouting what were presumably oaths in a language Edith did not recognize. Probably gibberish, no real language at all. She was a small woman, sturdily built, and she was wearing what she always wore, two huge spots of rouge and a short fur coat. Her hair looked as if it had been recently chopped at, or sawn off, Edith thought, with a dull knife. Edith had seen her around the neighborhood for months, and given her a wide berth.

Edith called to the waiter. "I think there is something floating in here," she said apologetically, holding up a pitcher of milk. This was her favorite waiter, the one she called Pablo because of his enormous burning dark eyes. Pablo frowned, and took the pitcher away. He returned moments later with sugar and a small vessel of cream. Edith didn't want cream. She never took cream, she wanted milk, and she already had sugar, but she decided to leave well enough alone. She would just drink her coffee black this morning, she wasn't really all that fussy, black with sugar. "Thank you," said Edith, but Pablo was looking over his shoulder at Esmerelda, who had stopped to search in a trash basket. "Crazy lady," said Pablo, tapping his head. "No-good lady." Edith didn't think you should blame someone for being crazy and she was sorry for Pablo that he had said such a mean thing. Especially not crazy in love, which was part of Esmerelda's problem, or at least the form it sometimes took. Edith shifted in her chair again and realized that the table where she was sitting was going to be uncomfortably close if Esmerelda stood outside Hector's Flower Store today. Edith glanced around for another place to sit, a table further away, but they were all occupied. The café had filled up. It was a lovely morning.

Why Esmerelda had fallen in love with Hector nobody seemed to know. Of course, nobody knew why anybody loved anybody. Or why anybody didn't, either, for that matter. Edith herself thought it must have to do with flowers. Maybe Esmerelda had loved a gardener in another land. Or maybe Hector had once given her an old corsage, something he had been going to throw away. Maybe he had pinned it on her coat to fulfill a bargain with God. You never knew. Hector had certainly been nice enough to send flowers to Edith when her mother died, even remembering that the old lady had loved freesias. You could fall in love with Hector and remain perfectly sane, Edith decided. She shut her eyes and tried unsuccessfully to imagine falling in love with Hector. When she opened them, she let out a little cry. Esmerelda was passing so close to Edith's table that Edith might have reached out and touched her sleeve. Her hideous ragged sleeve.

Esmerelda's coat was more dreadful close up than Edith could have imagined. There was a ghastly slickness to the fur, and the lining was torn and hanging down in front, and Edith wasn't a bit sure what kind of animal this fur had originally come from. It reminded her of some terrible red monkey, big as a child, balding in places. But Esmerelda was clearly an Eskimo, Edith decided, getting a good look at the woman's cheekbones. In which case it was no wonder she had gone crazy. You would have to be crazy not to go crazy if you were an Eskimo woman in New York City. Edith's heart was beating rapidly, but maybe she had only imagined the smell.

Edith patted her hair, straightened the collar of her nice

navy-blue jacket. She opened a napkin and put it in her lap. Esmerelda was now standing among the lilacs outside Hector's, and she was plucking at something on the front of her coat. She wasn't shouting or singing right now, and unless you saw her close up you might not know she was crazy. The only crazy person Edith had ever known had been her Aunt Neddie, and she had never wandered around shouting, or singing. "Neddie is not herself," Edith's mother sometimes said. Edith knew that Neddie had seen visions and heard voices, and they had not been friendly. Poor Neddie. She had perished so long ago, and in a far-off land, and Edith had not even been thirteen. Now that Edith's mother was dead there was nobody left to remember Neddie except Edith, and all Edith had were fragments, shards really, painful bits and pieces of a woman whose lipstick was too dark, whose kisses had always hurt Edith's cheeks, whose breasts had always been embarrassingly visible in her loose bathing suits, and whose favorite poem had begun, "O Western wind, when wilt thou blow," a poem that had meant nothing to Edith when Neddie had shown it to her years and years ago, weeping, when Edith had been eight.

Edith opened three sugars and put them in her coffee, but it was too much, and did not make up for the lack of milk. She knew most people did not like milk in espresso, but Edith did. She decided to call to Pablo. Pablo was

looking into the street, where Hector was crouched behind a blue van, waiting for Esmerelda to leave. Kind-
hearted, Hector never called the police. Instead, he hid.
Edith watched as Hector peeked around the back of the
vehicle and Edith waved a tiny wave at him, but he didn't
wave back. No doubt he hadn't seen her. Hector had a big
soft wife somewhere, Edith was sure of this, a nice wife
who cooked lamb for him, and orzo, and dropped cinna-
mon in all his food to give it mystery. Edith tried but failed
to imagine him in a house with furniture, she could only
picture him on the sidewalk surrounded by flowers, flowers of all kinds in all kinds of containers, big mayonnaise
jars of flowers.

Esmerelda began shouting and stamping, and waving
her arms. All around Edith people were talking and she
could catch nobody's eye. It wasn't easy to ignore Esmerelda all by yourself, and Edith rummaged in her bag
for her compact. She snapped it open and looked at herself in the mirror. There you are, she said under her
breath, there you are. Edith applied a few dabs of powder
to her nose and chin. It was so difficult to appear normal
at times like these. And nearly impossible not to stare, but
who knew? You might go crazy yourself. You might break
into song, or pull off your garments. You might run naked
down Broadway baying at the moon, or start directing
traffic. Yesterday she had caught herself talking out loud

to no one at the bus stop. "Lovely, lovely day," were the words Edith had heard herself saying. Innocent enough, but once you began, where might it end? Well, thought Edith, putting her powder back in her bag and glancing at Esmerelda. She would certainly never be crazy enough to wear that coat. Of course, maybe it was all the poor thing had. Maybe underneath that coat Esmerelda was wearing nothing at all. Edith shivered. She touched the top button of her nice silk blouse for reassurance. She smoothed her skirt. What would Edith do under those circumstances? Would Edith be able to stick her nice plump clean arms down those filthy sleeves to cover her nakedness? If she were thrown out on the streets could she wear filthy skins? Edith herself had never been dirty. During one regrettable period Edith had spent several days in her nightgown. It was after her mother died. She had felt odd for a day or two. Maybe a week or two. Edith didn't want to think about the odd feeling. It might come back.

Because who knew where crazy came from? It might just drop out of the sky.

"May I take this chair?" A young woman spoke to Edith. "Or are you waiting for someone?" She hovered politely at the edge of Edith's table. Startled, Edith jumped. She had been trying to remember whether it was locusts that John the Baptist had eaten.

"Oh no," said Edith, "I'm not waiting for anybody. Well,

not anybody in particular," she said. "I mean, I think we're all waiting for somebody or *other*," Edith went on. "We just don't know who it is." Edith shrugged helplessly. "You can take the chair," she added, as the girl remained poised with her hands on the back of it.

"Thanks," was all the girl said in reply, and she dragged the chair to a table nearby at which two and now three students were sitting. "He hates my guts," Edith heard one of them say. "He loves my guts," said another. Edith wondered of whom they were speaking. Could it be her Pablo? Edith glanced at him. He stood against the doorway, his arms crossed over his chest, ready to do battle with the crazy lady if need be. That seemed to Edith almost as terrible as being crazy. Why would you look forward to trouble?

Esmerelda began to sing. She started so softly that at first Edith couldn't be sure but she concentrated, and she turned her head in Esmerelda's direction, and yes, that soft crooning was Esmerelda singing. And she had really a surprisingly lovely voice. This was turning out to be an extraordinary morning, most extraordinary. Edith almost closed her eyes. And then Esmerelda ruined it with another shout. Edith pushed her chair back and signaled to Pablo for her check. Pablo misunderstood, bringing Edith another cup of coffee. "The check," she said to Pablo, "*l'addition*," and she scribbled in the air with an imaginary pen.

And then Esmerelda began singing again, but this time she kept it up, and her body began to move with the song and Edith felt like swaying too, like a big top-heavy flower on a stem. She could hear bits and pieces of "Blue Moon" riding somewhere under the surface of Esmerelda's voice, like something borne along by water. Edith found herself gripping the plastic arms of her chair, holding her breath, so as not to be carried away. It was a most unexpectedly pleasant feeling.

(For a time after Edith's mother's death, Edith had sat and clung to the arms of the old green chair, as if otherwise she might blow away, or be carried upward on a draft, as if she had no gravity of her own anymore, and when she had spoken out loud in the empty room her voice had seemed to come from a corner of the ceiling instead of her own body. She had been unable to move and had wondered briefly if it might not be due to the woodwork, which was so very dark, and she made plans to have it painted as soon as she could speak.)

Somebody applauded when Esmerelda finished her song. Edith saw Pablo, a sarcastic smile on his face, clapping in the doorway. Oh dear, thought Edith, but fortunately Esmerelda paid no attention. She turned to leave, blowing a kiss at the flower store, waving good-bye. Maybe she is in love with the flowers, thought Edith. Maybe it isn't Hector at all. As Esmerelda drew near the café again Edith picked up her coffee. She held the cup halfway to her lips, elbows resting on the table. She sat perfectly still, so as to be invisible. Esmerelda stopped right next to Edith's table. Edith could see the dangling lining of her terrible coat. "Miedabee," said Esmerelda. Her voice was hoarse. Miedabee? Edith began to lift the cup to her lips with an air of what she hoped was nonchalance, but her hands were shaking. "Miedabee," Esmerelda repeated, more urgently, and Edith found herself turning to look directly at Esmerelda and into her eyes, which were dark as cherries. "Mind the bee," said Esmerelda, pointing to Edith's cup. A yellow jacket sat on the rim, interested perhaps in Edith's lipstick.

"Oh," cried Edith, dropping everything. "Oh!" she cried, getting up from the table and waving her hands about, making a small commotion. Esmerelda nodded her head several times and then continued on her way. "Thank you very much," called Edith, but Esmerelda did not turn around. From the back, Esmerelda's coat looked almost jaunty. It rode up a bit, giving her an incongruously schoolgirl look. Half a block away, Esmerelda started shouting. "Well, that would have been really quite nasty," said Edith right out loud. "How terribly nice of that woman," Edith said next, somewhat more insistently, looking around to see if anyone had noticed. How pathetic the young are, thought Edith, so self-absorbed.

Hector now returned to his store, nodding and chatting with a few people who called out to him. He waved at Edith and she waved back. Everything seemed refreshed, like after a good rain. Edith paid her bill, leaving Pablo a good tip as usual, although he had fairly thrown the check on the table, scolding her, Edith knew, for speaking to the no-good lady. Edith strolled over to the flower store and bent down on the sidewalk and stuck her face in the flowers. She bought a large bouquet. Some of these she deposited carefully in the trashbasket on the corner where Esmerelda would be sure to find them. Lilacs. But there were still a great many flowers left, and these Edith carried home in her arms, already singing under her breath.

LEOPARD-SKIN SKIRT

THERE WAS THE sound of something ripping as Edith sat down, and each adjustment of her body produced further ripping sounds. Could it possibly be the material of the banquette on which she was now sitting? Edith very much hoped so. She tried a tiny experiment with her left leg, moving it infinitesimally to the right, really almost no more than flexing her thigh, and she heard material tear again. This was very bad. It was not the furniture.

Edith was thus paralyzed. She was sitting in the down-stairs lobby of the Angelika Theater, where she did not belong and should never have come, and now could not possibly leave. Ever. To make matters worse, there, across the room, she was quite sure, wait, she would put her glasses on, yes, she was certain she saw Ronald Colman, who had been an old beau of her mother's (or perhaps this was his son or grandson, Edith realized), but whoever he was he would be certain to have heard of her mother, and perhaps remember Edith herself, Edith as a small child, and Edith called out as genteelly as she could, "Mr. Colman?" and as he seemed to turn slightly at the sound of his name, and although she did not like to raise her voice she did, calling again, "Mr. Colman? Ronald? Is that you?" and then he disappeared with a tall woman wearing a green shawl.

The movie was about to begin and everyone but Edith rose to enter the small dark theater. The usher looked over at Edith and raised his eyebrows, holding open the door, and she had to shake her head with as much sophistication as she could, trying to imply with one brief shake that she had already seen the opening moments of this film and shared what was possibly his view that it wasn't worth seeing twice. Certainly not worth hurrying up off this nice comfy banquette to see twice. The usher waited another fraction of an instant and then he shrugged and stepped into the theater himself. Good. Edith was now alone. Bravely she put her hand round the back of her skirt, hoping it had been simply a belt loop tearing, that would be the best, the only acceptable damage, but alas her belt and both back loops were secure. But what they were holding up now seemed to Edith's timid explorations the equivalent of a grass skirt. The whole thing seemed to have disintegrated on Edith's body, every possible seam and dart. The material of the skirt itself was fast disappearing, like something in a laboratory experiment, as if Edith's skin and this particular fabric were at war and one must destroy the other. Some chemical reaction. Well, at least it was she who was winning because everywhere that Edith should have encountered skirt, Edith now felt only Edith.

Thank god she believed in decent underwear. Where had she gotten the idea that she needed to wear something daring, and go someplace different? What had possessed her? Here she was stuck in a disintegrating faux leopard-skin skirt, one hundred and seventy-five blocks from home, while a man who might conceivably have turned into the love of her life had slipped away before Edith had been able to introduce herself. Re-introduce herself. And now, how would she get out of here? Edith looked around to make sure she was alone, to make sure the refreshment stand people were busy with each other, which they were; this was one of the advantages of Edith's age and, it must be said, of her avoirdupois, and she stood up and tugged what was left of the back of her skirt round to the front. She examined herself and saw that if she held her pocketbook right in front, like one of those Scottish chiefs, and if she affected a sort of limp, she might just make it into the street and thence into the first cab she saw. No matter what kind of driver it was, she would get in. Even if he drove across three lanes of traffic to screech to a halt halfway up the curb, she would get in. She no longer cared. She nearly wept with frustration to think that there, in what she now thought of as the bowels of the earth, sat Ronald Colman, ignorant of Edith Tallmadge and their connection to each other. Edith limped to the glass doors, which she opened with her shoulder, and then she limped down the steps to the street, where she started to laugh, and couldn't stop, and every fresh burst of laughter created an accompanying sound of material tearing, and the more it tore the more she couldn't stop laughing, it really was terribly funny, and she hailed a cab and, holding onto what was left of her skirt, she climbed in, gave her address, and continued to laugh for several blocks before she took out her hanky and wiped her eyes. There must be something intrinsically funny about the sound of ripping cloth. First it scares you to death, and then you get used to it. This made Edith start laughing all over again. Then she realized, vexed at herself, that it had not been Ronald Colman at all but David Niven. "Niven, you idiot," said Edith to herself. Her mother had played opposite him in one of those most obscure British films in which her mother had been cast as a difficult heiress, which was exactly what her mother had been, come to think of it, among other things. Well, it had been David Niven and no wonder he hadn't come over. Stupidly, she hadn't recognized him without that little mustache. Or a son, of course, not the man himself. Or a cousin. Niven had become synonymous in Edith's mind with that pencil-thin mustache, that most discreet of little mustaches, a *niven* she might have preferred to call it, as *mustache* was a vulgar bushy word, something vaguely sexual about it, possibly with things stuck there, dangling off. Well, maybe it was all for the best. David Niven would never have looked twice at a ridiculous middle-aged woman in a leopard-skin skirt, although the taxi driver did, lingering while Edith and her bottom disappeared inside the big front door. "They don't make 'em like you anymore, lady," he might have hollered, but she had been too far away to hear. Thank god she was home, even if the old place was big now, and all the rooms echoed with the sound of her heels as she went up the wide front stairs.

TOTES

EDITH'S MOTHER NEVER used the word *pocketbook*. "It's a *handbag*, Edith, a handbag." But whatever you wanted to call it, Edith's was broken. The shoulder strap had worn out and broken in two. And it was her favorite pocketbook, roomy enough for ears of corn or cold roast chickens or beach towels, and although Edith did not carry such things, you never knew, and Edith couldn't part with it. Someday she might go on a picnic. She thought perhaps Rudy Cervantes of Cervantes Shoes might be able to fix it with a few stitches. She liked Rudy. He had said to her, "I was sorry to hear that your mother died." It was the lovely word *died* that did it to Edith, and she had found tears in her eyes. "Yes," Edith had said, "thank you." *Died* was a graceful, dignified word, and that was what her mother had done. She had died. *My mother died.* Edith had written the words on sheets of paper when she couldn't feel anything. *Mother died.* And then she could.

It was raining this morning and as Edith placed her bag on the counter she began to hiccup. What is the matter with me now, she thought. She held her breath until her face got red. She pretended to swallow nine times, a sure cure. She searched the bottom of her bag for a packet of sugar. *Hic.*

The sounds of tapping came sporadically from the back room and—could it be possible?—a woman's laugh. Edith blushed furiously. What was going on here? In a respectable shoemaker's establishment? Perhaps it was the radio. Then, instead of Rudy another man appeared at the counter.

"Oh," she said, her hand still rummaging through her pocketbook. What was she thinking? How could she leave her bag with anybody when she had not even cleaned it out? Her fingers encountered pens, paper clips, bus transfers, pennies. A folded copy of the Constitution that she had always meant to read sometime. And some sticky substance that was probably sugar. "Oh," she repeated.

"I am Rudy's nephew," he said, "Luigi. At your service, madam."

"Well," said Edith, "How very nice to meet you." *Hic.* She blushed. "Dry toast," she explained, "and it is raining." Then another hiccup. Edith wished she could disappear, as the last hiccup was one of those loud ones, so surprising that an old man reading the newspaper and having his shoes shined looked up.

Luigi was smiling. "I have just the thing," he said and produced from behind the counter a jar of murky-looking fluid in which what appeared to be smallish eyeballs were floating. Edith shrank back.

"Cherries," he said. "For ten years soaked in vodka.

Ready today, as luck would have it. They are only for emergencies, special occasions." And he dipped a small fork in and pulled one out for Edith. "Go ahead," he said. "Don't be shy. Eat." Edith hated to hurt anyone's feelings. She had good manners. The fire it lit in her mouth was delicious and oily and she thought she might have to sit down. "Oh my," she said a minute later, opening her eyes again.

"Now there will be no more hiccups," said Luigi.

Edith showed him the strap of her pocketbook. "I can do this for you while you wait," he said, his hand resting on one of Edith's fingertips. She withdrew it, being shy.

"Oh, that isn't necessary," she said. "I can come back."

"Perhaps you want to remove some things? Maybe your wallet and keys?"

"Oh, just my wallet and keys, yes. I forgot, just in case I have to go home, or buy something of course, one of my errands this morning," she said, blushing again. She didn't want him to think she thought he might steal something.

Luigi smiled. His teeth were nice. "It will be ready in ten minutes," he continued. "It is better you stay here— look at the rain and your shoes." He glanced meaningfully at Edith's new sandals, which were the Roman-slave type. She had bought them only yesterday. She had never worn anything like them before, although they probably did not go with the rest of her clothes.

"Oh no, I must fly," she said, waving her hand meaningfully, suggesting many errands that wouldn't wait. And then she sneezed.

He handed her a pair of Totes. "At least put these on," he urged.

"We don't *wear* Totes," her mother might have said. "We have our galoshes." But Edith thought it might be all right just once. She bought an umbrella too. There was something so nice about Luigi, even though he did smell a lot like aftershave.

Edith walked down the street. There was still a great deal of the day left. She stood in front of the window at La Rosita and watched the big white cakes go round on the revolving dessert stand. The small cups of flan. She held the door open for a young woman with a stroller. It was sunny now and the Totes on her feet felt warm, but she had no wish to hurt Luigi's feelings and she kept them on. Edith walked toward the decrepit old Woolworth's, where spring flowers were for sale on the sidewalk, placed on green stands that reminded Edith of baseball bleachers. Edith felt sorry for the plants, all a bit straggly from lack of pruning, and she bought a funny-looking fern. Halfway home, the fern in her arms, she imagined Luigi handing back her handbag all repaired and asking her to marry him in the same breath. She would have to decide in a split second, as such moments did not come twice in a life, but she already knew she would say yes.

FIG LEAF

FIFTY-FOUR AND Edith had never seen a naked man. Even Gloria Harris who was cross-eyed had seen a naked fellow even if he was just running down the street when she took her vacation in Paris. Or so she said, anyway. "It was flapping up and down like a little bitty frankfurter," Gloria had said to Edith and then giggled while Edith tried to look dignified. But the truth was Edith felt left out. It hit her all of a sudden that she might die without ever seeing how God created Man.

She decided to go to the Metropolitan Museum. She remembered being hurried past the Greek and Roman statues when she was a little girl, although as far as she could remember they had mostly had it broken off or had a leaf on top. She knew she could buy an anatomy textbook but she wanted to find the mystery uncovered in art. At least there would be a little atmosphere. A little bitty frankfurter. But when she got off the M4 bus she realized that it was Monday and the museums were all shut. Oh well, she thought, monkeys, and started to walk down to the zoo. It was a warm day and Edith removed her jacket. But the zoo was closed for repairs. So Edith bought herself a nice bacon sandwich at the Gardenia Restaurant, which didn't shoo you out at this hour, and then she went home.

There was a fuss on the first floor. Mr. Richards had somehow gotten loose again. The poor old man had suffered a stroke last year, and had lost the part of his brain that contained common sense. He was in the lobby wearing a towel as Edith came through the door and Edith nodded to him nicely. There seemed to be a good deal of soap still in Mr. Richards's hair. "You!" he shouted. "Who won the Battle of Thermopylae! None of these idiots seem to know." Edith swallowed: the towel was sliding off Mr. Richards's right hip, but just then the nurse came running pink-faced down the stairs. She ushered Mr. Richards into the elevator. "You've been a naughty boy!"

Later Edith took down the encyclopedia. "The Battle of Thermopylae," she wrote in her neat script, "was fought by the Persians and the Greeks. The Persians were the winners." She slid the note under Mr. Richards's door. The next morning he was back, ringing her bell. "You come into a room like the Spanish Armada, my dear," he said, looking her up and down with a practiced eye. Mr. Richards had once been quite the ladies' man. He winked. "You are a fine figure of a woman. My hat is off to you." And the hat, which had been covering the most important of the naked bits of Mr. Richards, was whisked away and Edith, astonished, stared. Well, she thought, so that's it.

It was a little sad, thought Edith. Not very useful looking. Of course she didn't permit herself much of a look;

she had turned quickly, or fairly quickly, and gone back inside, closing her door politely but firmly just as the nurse had appeared on the stairs again. "It is much too warm for a hat," she heard Mr. Richards protesting loudly a moment later, "Much too warm for a hat, goddamn it!"

They certainly had their hands full next door.

SUNGLASSES

EDITH'S MOTHER'S CAR had been kept in a garage all these years. It was a 1955 Buick Skylark, two-tone, white on top and red on the bottom. The insides were red leather and very comfy; a little tray for a Kleenex box was hidden under the dashboard and it swiveled out if you needed a good cry. It was in this car that Edith had learned to drive, and in this car that she and her mother had driven to the country in the summertime. They had even spent one week long ago on the banks of the Delaware River, where Edith had gone wading and later tried unsuccessfully to cook shad. When driving, Edith's mother insisted, Edith had to wear sunglasses. "Glare is the enemy of the safe driver," her mother had said. The sunglasses were tinted a dark blue, and Edith didn't like the way the world looked when she wore them. Nevertheless, when she decided to take the car out again, she put them on. She sat in the car in the dark garage. With its battery charged the motor started right away, and it only had twenty-five thousand miles on it, every one of them driven by Edith herself. The mechanic had offered to buy it from Edith should she ever want to sell. So had the man in the parking garage.

A Saint Christopher medal did not hang from the rear-view mirror. It was with a Saint Christopher medal that

Edith's mother had attempted to explain to Edith the concept of irony. The example her mother had given was that in the one accident she knew of the only injury done to the driver was from just such a medal, which had put out one of the driver's eyes. Her mother had relished the story. "It put his eye out, Edith. Other than that, he did not have a scratch. Now there is a perfect example of irony." Edith had nodded her head knowingly, but really it had taken her a long time to understand about irony.

It made her nervous at first, driving out of the city. She was afraid it would revive old memories of her mother in happier days. She decided to drive without the glasses. Even if it made her sad, she wanted to see what the world looked like.

SHOES

ON MOST SATURDAYS since her mother had died, Edith had taken to driving into the country. She left early, right after her cup of tea (Edith was not partial to a big breakfast), and seldom had any particular plan. Sometimes she packed a sandwich or a piece of fruit. Today, she had taken the highway that went out past the closed-down factory on her way to Lambertville (there was a waterfall near Lambertville somewhere) but instead, on an impulse, she had followed a series of cardboard arrows that had brought her to a small house in the woods, a cabin really. A sign on old construction paper read simply HERE. TODAY. She slowed and stopped. There were a number of things in the yard, some broken furniture, a table and three wooden chairs, a battered chest of drawers, as well as a great many sheets and blankets, several towels, and a certain number of what appeared to be clothes draped over the porch railing. Ordinarily Edith would not have stopped at a place like this, but there was something glittering on a rack on the front yard that she just had to see. Without her good glasses she couldn't make out anything except the colors, orange, red, green, and a curious midnight blue. It looked like a shoe rack. She parked her car and got out cautiously, smoothing her skirt as she stood there, looking first toward the bright objects and then, upon hearing banging, toward the house.

On the front porch a man was kneeling over what appeared to be a screen door, a hammer in his hand. She coughed politely. He was wearing a pair of yellow boots, and he looked young from the side but when he straightened up Edith saw he was probably close to seventy. He had blue eyes and his hair was sandy going gray, and as he looked at her Edith noticed that his hands were enormous, much too big for an older person. The hammer looked tiny in his grasp. Edith blushed; she felt ridiculously prim in her gray skirt and white blouse with the Peter Pan collar and her sensible shoes that laced. Well, she was who she was, nothing to be done about it. "I saw your signs," she began. She walked a few steps toward the shoe rack, and her left hand was touching one beautiful bright orange dancing shoe. What an extraordinary collection! They were all high heels and open toes, they had delicate yet sturdy straps, and they were such marvelous glittery colors.

"Wife put them up," he said. "You're early."

"Well, I hope not too early," said Edith. She found herself trembling with pleasure over these shoes, but she did check her watch. Actually it was rather early. It was only seven-thirty. She looked at him again. His overalls were of a liverish color and the blue shirt he wore underneath was missing all its buttons, or at least all of them that Edith could see. She noticed, with a start, that his fly was open. It wasn't exactly a fly, but those big snaps. He was not looking at her anymore, thank goodness, and she turned away hurriedly. It would be impossible for Edith to meet his eyes now and when he spoke again she tried to look at the clapboard behind his head, up where the porch roof met the siding, but she saw a hornet's nest there, which unnerved her, and everything was so sadly peeling. Edith thought of getting back into her car and driving away but that would be embarrassing.

"Long as you're here you might as well take a look around," he offered. "Help yourself. I don't see a crowd waiting at the gate." He bent back to his work.

Edith approached the porch. She touched a few of the garments lying atop the old blankets on the railing. There were a number of sweaters with beads sewn in, from long ago days, and a few sweatshirts. There was a small plaid dress and a fake leather jacket with fringe, suitable for a little girl. There was also a pink tutu and several pairs of pink tights, all of them with stained feet. Edith had only wanted to see the shoes but she thought it was impolite not to look at everything.

A thin tired-looking woman came through the door to the porch, and she took the tights out of Edith's hands. "These are not for sale," she said, frowning. Edith had only been touching them. "Well, all right," said Edith. "They're probably too small for my niece anyway, although she does love to dance." The woman didn't say anything and Edith continued. "Of course she's just starting, and it's nothing fancy, just ballroom dancing. I admit it's very old-fashioned. Not like children you hear about today." Edith smiled and stopped. She had grown uncomfortable. She didn't have a niece! She had made one up on the spot! She hoped they wouldn't ask her niece's name as she didn't know what she would say. But the woman didn't ask her anything. Instead, her hand rummaged in her apron pocket and withdrew a paper napkin and a tiny toy rabbit. Her face was pale and her hair the color that is no color at all. She wiped her face with the napkin, and disappeared back into the house, the pink tights in her arms.

Edith looked at some household utensils. A rusty egg-beater, a chipped bowl, a set of nesting bowls with the small red one missing. Edith knew this because Edith had a full set of well cared for nesting bowls in which she beat her eggs and let her bread rise, in which she made her batters for cakes and stirred her puddings. Even now, with her mother gone, Edith continued to bake.

"Cleaning out the room," said the man, kneeling over the door frame and unrolling a large piece of screen. He had a staple gun in his hand now and it made sharp satisfying sounds as he stapled the screen into place. "Most of the furniture went last week. Can't keep this stuff forever, I told her." Several plastic dolls poked out of a cardboard box which the man shoved over to Edith with his foot. "How old's your little girl?"

"Well," Edith began, "she's not exactly my little girl."

The woman reappeared at the door. She looked at Edith, her eyes pink, then came out onto the porch again. She stooped and picked up the box of toys and she carried the box indoors under her arm.

"You going to keep everything?" The old man sounded impatient. "All this junk?"

"Nina might want them." The woman stood in the doorway.

"Nina doesn't want them. She wants new." The old man shook his head.

Edith began to feel peculiar. She knew she should get to the point. "I'm sorry," she said. "I didn't mean to be worrying your wife. I was just looking at the shoes anyway. Hildegarde loves to play dress-up and dance. She really just loves to dance. She loves Ginger Rogers, although for myself I like Cyd Charisse. She was the partner Fred Astaire preferred, if I recall correctly." Edith blushed and went on blushing.

"Never heard of either one," said the old man. "I never did dance."

Edith collected herself. She patted the front of her

jacket and smoothed back her smooth hair. Thinking about Fred always made her feel like a big flower. "Well, Hildegarde would just have the best time with those shoes," she repeated. "Are the shoes for sale?" asked Edith, just out of curiosity.

"Nobody around here to wear them anymore," said the man. "Belonged to the wife's daughter and she ran off six months ago." He grunted. "Not that it's any of your business."

"No, I'm sure it isn't," said Edith, nodding her head, and touching her hair with one hand. She had recently done the bluing thing to it and she was glad as it made her feel respectable and grown-up. It made for a nice barrier between her and whatever this old man was living his life about. An old dog, mostly beagle, limped across the dirt and slid under the porch. "Good-for-nothing mutt," said the man good-naturedly. "Ran down to North Carolina, she did," he continued. "I know because we got a card. If you're interested you can have them for, I don't know. Five dollars?" He shook his head. "Don't know who'd want them, myself. But the girl spent a lot on them. Got to ask the wife." He had the screen door on its end now and was attempting to fit it back on its hinges. His back was to her, thank goodness. Edith's eyes strayed to a cardboard box full of picture frames. Some of them contained pictures still, and she reached for one with a photo of a serious little girl with crooked teeth. She bent down and picked it up. The cheap wooden frame was painted with what appeared to be red nail polish. She was looking into the girl's face when the man startled her again. "That's her," he said. "That's her when she was a little thing. You should have seen her a couple years later. Makeup? She grew up quick. That was the problem." He came and stood next to Edith, she could hear him breathing. He took the picture out of her hands and placed it on the aluminum chair by the side of the door. "Didn't mean for that to find its way out here," he said, without further explanation. He turned back to the door and began hammering the bolts down into the hinges he'd lined up. Then he closed the screen door and wiped his hands on the sides of his overalls. He put the staple gun on the windowsill and put the hammer in his pocket.

Somewhere inside there was the sound of a television turned on and Edith heard a clatter of pans in the kitchen. From the back came the sounds of barking. "Carl?" called out a woman's voice. "You got the dog?"

"Under the porch," he yelled back. "Door's hung. Come take a look."

The woman came outside again. In her thin arms she was carrying a big paper sack. She didn't say anything to her husband but spoke instead to Edith. "Did you pass a green Chevy Caprice parked on Route 118 today? Near the turnoff to the lake?"

"No, oh dear, I didn't." said Edith. "I didn't come from Briscoe."

"There's a girl living right in that car. You drive by you give her these apples, will you?"

Edith hadn't time to answer before the woman handed her the paper sack.

"We saw her yesterday, but he"—she pointed at Carl—"wouldn't stop. I wanted to stop but he wouldn't do it. Next time we went by with some sandwiches but she wasn't there. It was a green car, old Chevy. She moves it around from place to place. You've seen it?" The woman seemed to have forgotten Edith's answer.

"No, I'm afraid I haven't. I'm not from around here. This is just what I do on the weekends." The woman's eyes were so dark as to be almost black. Edith didn't see a pupil anywhere in those eyes. "But if I see her I'll stop. Certainly."

"I'd be obliged," said the woman. "Just if you give her these apples. They are washed and ready for eating. If she's not in the car you can leave them on the hood, I guess. I put a roll of toilet paper and some napkins in there too. Don't know how a girl lives when she takes to living in a car."

"It's not the way we do things around here," muttered the old man. "Nobody lives in a car around these parts." He was sitting in the aluminum chair now, the picture in his lap.

"If you don't see her you can keep the apples yourself," said the woman.

"How much for the shoes, Lil," asked Carl. "The lady here is interested in them shoes."

"Those shoes?" Edith held her breath as the woman's eyes bored into her. "I got to get ten-fifty for the lot."

Edith put the apples down on the floor. "Well, that sounds very reasonable," she said, and she reached into her purse for the money.

"That's a genuine bargain," the woman said, her lips tight.

"Oh, I know," said Edith, handing her two five-dollar bills and a fifty-cent piece. "I'll go get them," she said and went down to gather them off the rack.

"Do they fit right?" asked the woman when Edith returned to the porch. "Did you try them on?"

"Oh, they're not for me," said Edith quickly. "They're for my niece." But she did sit down on the top step and remove her right shoe. She was wearing stockings even though it was a warm day, and she slid her foot easily into the orange dancing shoe. They might have been made for her. "She's going to be a big girl, tall like me," said Edith happily. "I'm sure they'll fit her fine." The woman nodded although she didn't smile and packed the shoes in a shopping bag and then she went inside.

Suddenly a little girl came running toward the porch, a big man running after her. The girl ran right up the steps and stood next to Edith, one grubby hand holding onto Edith's skirt. This startled Edith. It had been some time since anybody had grabbed hold of her. Edith thought the child might be four years old. "I said get over here," said the man, who Edith saw now was little more than an overgrown boy. The word *punk* came into Edith's mind.

The girl shook her head. She was wearing a blue dress. The hem was coming down in the front, Edith noticed, and the buttons were torn off in the back so the dress hung off one shoulder. Edith reached down and put her hand on the child's head. It was warm and sweaty and unlike anything else Edith had ever touched.

"Don't be grabbing the lady," said the boy with a glance at Edith. He looked angry.

"Oh no, it's quite all right, she reminds me very much of my niece. Just so full of mischief." Edith stopped herself, conscious of prattling.

"Did you do this, Nina?" he asked the child, coming closer and holding up a bit of cloth with a knot tied in the middle. His face looked so red. The child moved closer to Edith, popping her thumb into her mouth. "Did you do this to my shirt?" The old woman came out and pried the child away, taking her indoors with her. The boy went inside too and Edith could hear arguing, and then the back door slammed.

"Son-in-law. Wife's daughter's husband. Hard to believe, isn't it? He's no more than a brat himself." The old man was speaking freely now. "He didn't treat her good and she ran right off. What a mess, eh? Left the little girl behind, too."

"I am so sorry to hear it," said Edith, who was.

"Well, none of your worry."

Edith said she had to be going. She said she didn't need any help with her packages. She picked up her bag of shoes with one hand and her sack of apples in her other and went toward her car. Before she left, the woman ran down the porch steps and across the yard to her. Edith had just gotten in the car.

"If you see her, give her this." The woman pressed a twenty-dollar bill into Edith's hand.

"Oh no, I couldn't," said Edith. "What if I don't see her?" But the woman was already halfway back to the house. Edith saw how thin and white her legs were.

"All right," said Edith to herself. "If I see her I will. I'll save it till I see her." She looked in her bag for the car key. But now the old man was coming across the yard toward the car. He was wiping his neck with a red cloth.

"Hold up," he called, although Edith had not yet put her key in the ignition. He leaned down to speak to Edith in a whisper. "Give her this if you see her." Close up, his face filling her window, he seemed much older than before, and Edith saw how his mouth trembled when he talked, as if his lips might shake loose. He handed Edith a five and three creased one-dollar bills. "Last time we heard she was on Route 118 in a little lay-by," he said. Edith nodded. "And here," he said, "something for your little niece." He reached into his pocket and took out a pair of pink sunglasses with rhinestones glued above the lenses.

"Oh," said Edith, taking them from his hand. "Well, thank you so much." The old man nodded, and backed away from the car.

As she drove toward Briscoe Edith searched the highway for signs of the Chevy Caprice. When she got to the lay-by she pulled over and parked, but there were no other cars. She pressed her palm to her face and tried to remember the hot-hair smell of a little girl. She closed her eyes. It had been so long since Edith was a little girl. Once her baby sister Rose had been missing for hours and everyone had looked for her. It was Edith who had found her in the attic. Forty years ago? She had been eating the sequins off a dress she'd found hanging there. Edith had tasted one or two sequins to make sure they weren't poison, then she had led the child into the bathroom and washed her face.

Later Edith stopped in a diner (The Starlite) and asked if anybody had heard of a girl who was living in a Chevy Caprice. The old waitress just shook her head. Edith decided to call it a day. When she got back to the garage she sat in the car, thinking. Maybe tomorrow she would drive out again, take another look. She decided to keep the sunglasses in the glove compartment and she put the twenty-eight dollars under the backseat, where she would always have it handy should she run into the girl. Then she picked up her bag of apples and her bag of shoes and went home.

That night, before retiring, Edith tried on her new shoes. Sliding her feet in and buckling the straps (Edith had lovely feet, they were her best feature with her high arches and slender ankles) she thought of the girl whose shoes these had been, the girl who ran away. She thought of the girl in the car. She thought of Hildegarde, who didn't exist. At ten-thirty, Edith put on her music. The record was scratchy, the voice familiar, unmistakable. She hesitated. Then Edith stood up in her big white nightie and her orange glitter shoes, and began to dance.

SHOPPING BAG

EDITH PICKED UP her mother's ashes from the funeral parlor one sunny afternoon and carried them all the way home. They were quite heavy after all, but she carried them fifty-seven blocks, thinking to herself, Here's Zabar's, Mother, and here's the Town Shop, where our underwear comes from, don't you know, and here is where Teacher's was that had the good eggs Benedict. And across the street is where we like the iced coffee and the movie theater used to be and now there is another one. And here we are passing Williams Bar-B-Que Poultry and now across the street is Liberty House and here is where we bought the air conditoner thirty years ago and there was a bookshop here once too. And there is the old man to whom we always gave money and I will again, and in another couple of blocks, past the other good coffee place (Turkish) and falafel and nearer to La Rosita but first here is Straus Park and let's us sit down. Edith sat on a bench near the Queen Anne's lace (her mother's favorite flower) holding the pale blue shopping bag (Compliments of Riverside Chapel) that contained the cardboard box that contained her mother and held it on her lap like a baby. Edith placed the bag logo inward as she didn't want to attract sympathy on the street.

That night Edith dreamed she was wearing black clothes. She dreamed her mother's funeral was at the Metro Theater, with those steep seats, and as she passed her mother's body she wept, although she pulled herself together since people were looking. Her mother, though, was not behaving in manner befitting the dead. She insisted on trying to get out of the coffin. It took several people to hold her down (all of them strangers to Edith). It was all terribly sad and hard to understand. Finally Edith took her mother's arm and helped her up and together they walked into the lobby. Her mother was pleased and began to tell Edith a rhyme, which Edith couldn't hear. Still, they had a pleasant time standing there together in the lobby and then her mother vanished into the street.

If my mother isn't dead, thought Edith in the dream, whose ashes do I have?

BIRTHDAY SUIT

EDITH STOOD IN front of the mirror in her underwear. "You are an anomaly," said Edith to her reflection, the word sounding large and white and softish. *Fat* had never been a word Edith abhorred. Au contraire. She always rather liked the soft lapping sound of it, as something wonderfully reassuring. Edith surveyed her own vast expanse. Edith wore large white underpants (big as a sail on the shower rod), and what her mother called a good serviceable bra, which meant that it, too, was white and no-nonsense. Nothing sexy or disturbing in Edith's undergarments. All the words for fat were nice, thought Edith. *Plump,* for instance. Could there be a more good-natured word? She turned sideways to look at herself from another angle. *Heft.* Well, that wasn't so nice but at least it demanded respect. *Fatty* was not nice, but that was in the eye of the beholder and not Edith's problem. *Dumpling.* Now there was a nice word.

Edith felt hot. She took off her underthings and lay down on her big bed. I am a territory, Edith decided, running her hand over her rib cage. Virgin territory, not yet explored. I am wilderness. Nobody has put a flag here. Briefly Edith imagined a little American flag fluttering above. I am my own domain, but mostly unsettled. Edith closed her eyes and imagined tiny populations swarming over her body, setting up camp on the vast white moon of her stomach, scrambling for purchase, unrolling bedrolls, afraid of the winds at night. "*Oh ridiculous,*" said Edith out loud and got up and got dressed. It was time to go out.

UNDERWEAR

NO MATTER HOW hot the day, Edith wore all her underwear. That was what had kept her mother going so long, Edith knew, the fact that even when she was sick Mother did not just lie around in nightclothes. As long as she could stand, Mother wore everything a lady wore. Summer and winter. Garments for all seasons. Edith did the same. Ritual and discipline were important in a woman's life and Edith didn't want to lose her mind. Yesterday on the bus Edith had seen an old man write the word BUTTER three times in a blue notebook and Edith wondered what it would be like when she could no longer be sure of carrying the word *fish* in her head long enough to buy some. As if the word could slip away, swim back to some dark place, some liquid grotto in her brain, and Edith would be there in the street with no idea what she was about and have to go home empty-handed or with some unwanted purchase. A cellophane bag of balloons, say. Who knew what the mind might come up with? For this reason today Edith had written her grocery list on a salmon-colored index card, and placed it in her pocket. It was not too early to cultivate careful habits. "Capers?" she had written in her small neat print right under "Nice piece of fish" and "Lemon," and out she went fully clad.

Now, having successfully accomplished her shopping, Edith was carrying one-half pound of halibut, two plump lemons, and a narrow green jar of capers. She nodded to the doorman, whose name she couldn't remember because he was new, and walked into the back of the lobby and got in the elevator. She pressed 7 and the doors closed and with a familiar little lurch the car started its upward path. When the elevator came to a stop Edith stood waiting for the door to open but nothing happened. She looked at the rows of buttons and pressed 7 again. Nothing happened again. She pushed OPEN DOOR. Nothing. She looked above the door, where a passenger could note the elevator's progress, and two numbers were lit, 5 and 6. That was unusual. What did it signify? She hopped, as if to give the elevator a jump start, but nothing. The elevator didn't budge. Was she stuck between floors?

At the word *stuck*, Edith felt what she called a frisson of fear, but being a grown woman, she clenched the fingernails of her left hand into her palm and cleared her throat. She realized the humming of the tiny fan set in the ceiling had stopped and in its place was more silence. "Oh dear," said Edith in a whisper, "where am I?" She looked at her watch, (two forty-two) and then held it against her ear for the nice reassuring little ticks. Well, at least that was working. Edith pushed 6. Nothing happened. She pushed 5, then 6: ditto. She pushed them simultaneously. She spoke aloud, one hand on the collar of her coat, saying jovially, "What's going on here?" and the sound of her own voice followed by silence was disconcerting. She wanted to call down to the doorman in case he could hear her five flights up the shaft, but what could she call him? Yoo-hoo? She pushed the red alarm button and the faintest of bells sounded weakly and then died out. Somehow this frightened Edith more than anything.

"Oh dear," she said, and then, "oh dear, oh *dear.*" Edith began to feel terribly warm. "ALL RIGHT!" she roared, surprising herself with the hugeness of her own voice, then addressed herself more quietly: "Take off your coat." Immediately, Edith felt calm. She removed her coat and hung it over the railing along the back wall of the elevator. So that's what this is for, she thought. It had always reminded her of a ballet school barre. Edith looked at her watch again. Two forty-four? Edith felt a strong need to raise her voice again. "GOOD WORK!" she shouted. "Good work," she repeated. "Now what? Get hold of yourself, Edith. Concentrate. Read something." She took the list out of her pocket. "Yes," she said, "capers," and she reached into the paper bag. "Capers, check. Halibut? Halibut, check. Lemons. Lemons. I can always bite into a lemon if I go crazy," she reassured herself, "and snap out of it."

It was disagreeably warm now without the fan, and

after another flurry of unanswered calls for help she began to cry. "Stop it, Edith," she scolded herself. "Remove your outer garments." She undid her top button (rich man) and then she undid another (poor man), letting her fingers graze the soft collar of her cream-colored blouse. It was her second nicest blouse, silk and soft to the touch like the inside of a puppy's mouth. Edith undid a third button (beggarman), and then she buttoned them all up again. Then she unbuttoned all seven buttons (merchant) and let her blouse fall open. That was much better. She didn't want to marry a merchant, however, that sounded so boring, so she undid the button of her skirt. Chief. She was not the sort of woman a person asked to marry, being nearly six feet tall and plain-featured although full-figured, as they say. She was wearing, of course, a very pretty slip and her bra and garter belt and girdle and stockings. She fanned herself with the index card. She took several deep breaths. "I CAN'T STAND THIS!" yelled Edith, but only twice. There was no reply of any kind. Perspiring now, Edith pulled the blouse entirely out of the waistband of her skirt and then she undid the zipper. Help," she called, and pounded on the door but only scared herself worse. She stepped right out of her skirt. "I HAVE GOT TO GET OUT OF HERE," she said, hanging her skirt over the rail. "I MUST," she went on, kicking her shoes off, "OR MY FISH WILL SPOIL!" The bag of fish was on the floor. She wiped her face with the hem of her slip. A voice sounded through the door. "Is anybody there?" "Oh yes," shouted Edith eagerly. "I'm in here and the elevator is stuck, and—," but she was interrupted by banging. "Where is that confounded elevator!" shouted an old man's voice and Edith recognized the voice of 6B, who was hard of hearing. He must be hitting the door with his cane. The noise went on a long time, followed by silence. Edith had a terrible thought. Was she imagining this? What if she had already gone crazy? What if this were not an elevator at all but a cell in an asylum? But there were no furnishings of any kind and no window, no slot through which a prisoner could receive food or mail.

Edith began shrieking, "GET ME OUT OF HERE," but the panic passed, like weather in Colorado, where you could see rain in the distance hanging out of clouds like a Portuguese man-of-war forty miles away. Was it Colorado? She began shouting again and banging.

"You are in no danger," a male voice boomed from above. "Stay calm and I'll have you out of there in no time."

"Somebody better come soon because I'm taking all my clothes off," cried Edith, but there was no further communication. "Are you still there?" she asked, but heard only the high-pitched whine of some kind of machine and a renewed banging somewhere else. Big tears squeezed out of Edith's eyes and she reached down and gathered her slip to pull it over her head. There. Then she undid one front garter and one back garter. Edith had always loved the way garters worked. So efficient, and she loved bunching the stocking together behind the little doodad. She slid a stocking down one plump white leg, and then she slipped the the other stocking down. She reached behind her carefully and unfastened the hooks of her bra, feeling it loosen and letting the straps slide forward down her arms, and there were her breasts free and looking quite as they always had, large and plump and floury. She threw her bra on top of the pile of clothes on the floor. *Bang bang bang* went something somewhere. The air felt nice on her body. It was like skinny-dipping, which Edith had only done once many years ago because of the necessity of doing it at night and Edith not liking the look of lakes at night or the ocean either. But the water had felt startlingly good and she had never forgotten it, so refreshing, like being a fish. "Fish," thought Edith happily, and she considered unwrapping that too but instead removed her pearls and the little garnet earrings and placed them neatly on the floor atop her clothes.

At that moment the elevator began to move. There she was, keeping herself company, when the elevator doors opened on a big man with *Otis Elevator* written on his pocket. He looked at Edith and did not look away. "Well, I'll be," he said, and his smile was so infectious that Edith had to laugh. "It was so hot, Otis," she said, and stepped out. He caught her in his arms.

NO POCKETBOOK

ANOTHER HOT DAY and Edith is walking around with what she calls a snootful of tears. Her mother had repeated so many times in the last weeks when she was delirious, "I love you, I love you," and Edith had looked around wondering whom her mother could possibly have meant and it has begun to dawn only recently on Edith that she'd meant Edith.

Crossing Broadway at 103rd Street she sees a girl sitting on the bench eating a lollipop. Not a girl, a young woman of perhaps eighteen? Twenty? It is so hard to tell. She has long red hair and a stretchy top on and is wearing only a pair of shorts and no shoes. No shoes! She has toenail polish on but her feet look dusty. She looks familiar. Doesn't she live across the street? Edith has seen her grow up, hasn't she?

Edith is shy, but impulsively she sits down next to her. The girl keeps sucking away at the lollipop, now and then brushing her cheeks free of tears. She has no shoes and no pocketbook. Unable to speak, Edith gets up and hurries into the bagel store and returns with a bagel and cup of coffee with milk and sugar to give the girl. She won't have to say anything, she can just leave it on the bench beside her. "There's a little something for you," she can say. Then she will ask her if she needs anything else. It wouldn't be so terrible. Mother left so many clothes and the girl might sleep in the spare room for a night or two. What would be the harm? At first she thinks she must have misremembered which street, was it 103rd or 104th? The girl is gone. Vanished. There is nothing left of her but the lollipop stick.

BUNNY'SSISTER

1

BUNNY STANDS BY the side of the road in the middle of nowhere. It is dark and rainy. She isn't soaked yet—she fished out her tarp just as the first big drops came down —but she's thirsty from all those cookies. *Boom.* Thunder. It is raining harder now. In the distance she can hear the sound of a car and as its headlights appear she steps back among the trees. From where she is standing the car looks like a station wagon. Bunny doesn't know anybody who owns a station wagon but she thinks next time she'll wait for one of those. It would have a family person driving it for sure. The car passes, its tires making that sad swishing on the wet road. Bunny waves in the dark.

She likes the sound of the wind. Rain patters on her head too, and clicks all over the tarp. Maybe she can spend the night in the woods somehow. She certainly isn't about to climb into another car yet, not after Gary. God. He hadn't done anything to her, only himself, that was lucky. He made sad noises, as if he were crying, but he wasn't crying. He was jerking off. Then he wiped himself. She hadn't felt sick until he'd stuffed the tissue in the ashtray. "That's all right, you go ahead," Gary had said while she leaned her head out the window and heaved, but he hadn't patted her on the back. He didn't like to touch people. He had offered to drive her to the train station, and tried to give her a twenty-dollar bill, but she had decided to take her chances in the woods. "Suit yourself," said Gary, and had driven away. She had watched his red tail-lights disappear around the curve.

Bunny adjusts the tarp to keep the rain from running down her neck. She isn't sure how long she's been standing here. She isn't even sure which side of the river she's on because Gary kept going over all these bridges but maybe it was the same bridge. Maybe he had just driven around in circles. Maybe if she stands really still she can hear her mother calling her. Ha ha. *Boom* again. The wind whips the tarp around and Bunny's feet are cold. She has her worst sneakers on, the pink ones, and no socks. She hadn't thought about taking extra clothes. Her ankles are wet, the cuffs of her jeans. The grass is tall where she's standing, if it is grass; maybe it could be flowers. Queen Anne's lace. Lightning again, Bunny can see people hunched down next to trees. The hairs on the back of Bunny's neck prickle. She searches with her right hand in the jean-jacket pocket under the tarp. Her tiny scissors are still there, her embroidery needles and thread. The point of the scissors makes a reassuring prick on her index finger, her thumb. She pricks each finger in turn, and the thumb twice for good luck. The rest of the hash brownies are in her knapsack, wrapped up in tin foil. She should never have had even one bite. That's why she keeps think-ing midgets are staring at her. God.

She tries to imagine her mother looking worried and calling "Bunny!" in a scared way. But her mother would have to lean her head out the window and nobody would hear her above the Broadway traffic. Bunny tilts her head now, trying to direct the stream of water running down her cheek into her mouth. If only she had a cup. Bunny had volunteered to make breakfast this morning because it was her mother's birthday. That was how everything started. Bunny had a present for her mother. She had made it herself, an embroidered jacket, and it had her mother's name, Bernice, and also Bunny's and Merle's and flowers entwining everything. Bunny had thought about Merle when she made it; that was why it was so good, unicorns and sunbursts and rainbows and shooting stars. It used to be Merle's, but Merle hadn't finished embroi-dering it. So it was from both of them in a way. But Bunny didn't give it to her. Mook had come into the kitchen and Momma had put the unopened present back on the table while she jumped up. "Look who's here!" And it turned out Mook was about to install wall-to-wall carpeting for Momma and air-conditioning and they were going to clear out Merle's room and Bunny said, "But where will she stay when she comes home?" Momma stopped smil-ing. "Jesus Christ, Bunny," she had whispered and then

gone into her room and closed the door. Mook had followed her, and after a while music came drifting out and
Bunny knew they'd be in there for hours.

Then it was like God sent a spotlight down and it made
a big circle around her feet like a clown in the circus and
the idea came into her head to run away. She didn't make
any noise except that she was crying like an idiot for no
reason and then she calmed down. She made baloney
sandwiches. She packed her knapsack with a box of Mal-
lomars and the sandwiches. She took the money out of
the desk and she took all the laundry quarters. That was
for making calls from the road if she needed to. Then she
looked around and it seemed as if she'd never even lived
there and so Bunny just started emptying stuff on the
floor. Sugar and flour and coffee and a whole box of rice
and then a can of old chocolate syrup on top of that. It
scared her, but once she had started it was hard to stop.
She ripped open TV dinners and frozen peas and dumped
them too. She unrolled all the toilet-paper rolls and spread
them over the living room and kitchen. It was a mess.
Then she stole the hash brownies. Bunny's mother would
freak when she saw the kitchen but what she'd miss most
were the brownies.

Bunny starts to giggle but stops because it sounds so
noisy in the woods. Nothing else is making a sound except water dripping from the leaves. She wishes she had

a cigarette. And it's nice how fresh the woods smell but there isn't anyplace to sit. Bunny thinks there is a gas station a little way back where Gary stopped for gas and she got out to pee. If the bathroom door isn't locked she could spend the night in there. Then tomorrow figure out what next. She doesn't really have a plan. For a terrible second she doesn't know which direction she came from but then remembers. Left. Bunny still feels like something might be watching her but nothing is. Those are stumps and shadows and bushes. If she were home there would be sirens and horns honking and music in the hotel down the block. Bunny thinks for moment about her bed but then dismisses the thought. She doesn't want to go back. She is on her way.

THE DOOR ISN'T locked. It sticks but she gives a hard push. That is a good omen, and she goes inside and takes a long drink of water from the tap without turning the light on. Then she stands up straight, sighs, and wipes her chin on the back of her hand. Stepping back outside she can see a light is still on in the office, and the man is still there, his feet propped on the desk. As she stands there watching he stretches and yawns and looks at his watch. He takes one foot off the desk and then the other and after a second he stands up. She sees him light a cigarette (Bunny wishes she had a cigarette) then he puts on a jacket that is hanging off the back of the chair. He looks around, turns off all but one little light, and locks the gas station door behind him. Bunny is crouched behind a bush. He is humming something. Bunny hopes he doesn't check everything before he takes off. He doesn't; he gets in his car and he drives away. For just a second Bunny sort of misses him.

Bunny waits until she has counted to fifty. Then she stands up, takes her tarp off, and shakes it before stepping back inside the bathroom. It takes her a while to remember the light switch is a string hanging down. She doesn't want to leave the light on too long, but she needs to make sure the bathroom floor is okay, nothing disgusting anywhere before she settles down.

There is a lock on the door, a hook and eye, and she hooks it behind her. Some water has leaked under the door from the rain. Muddy footprints surround the sink, the toilet. There are a few paper towels on the back of the toilet but mostly it is that hot-air dryer that you're supposed to do your hands on. She could use it to dry out her ciggybutts if she had any. But even then she doesn't have matches. She should have stolen Gary's lighter. It was lying on the dashboard, she stared at it the whole time he was doing himself. Spanking his monkey, ha ha. Bunny shakes her head. There is her lipstick heart on the mirror that she drew there hours ago. Was it hours ago? Has anybody been in here since then?

She bends over the sink and takes another drink of water and then she rubs her finger over her teeth. Somebody else must have been here because there are two long brown hairs in the sink. Bunny rinses them down the drain. She takes her eyeliner out of a pocket in her knapsack and does her lower lid first, then her upper, then frowns and touches up her eyebrows a little. Bunny's eyebrows aren't any good. They don't arch and you can hardly see them. What she wants is to have eyebrows that look like a wolf, or some other kind of wild animal. Her eyes are boring and her hair is boring and her nose is too big and she wants to get it fixed sometime and she has a little tiny mouth. Well, not tiny, but she really does need lipstick or she is just so washed out. She frowns at her reflection in the mirror. She needs to get some waterproof mascara and some waterproof eyeliner too. Maybe blue. She looks better with eye makeup. Gary wouldn't have done anything if she'd looked older. Bunny looks twenty when she is fixed up. Although she is fourteen she is quite mature.

Now Bunny looks at the floor carefully. Then she wets some paper towels and wipes up everything she can see. A few hairs. She takes off her sneakers and lays them on the back of the toilet and she rinses her feet with warm water and soap and dries them with toilet paper. Finally she takes the tarp and shakes it out the door again, turning off the light in case somebody drives by. She is wearing the jacket she didn't give her mother. It is beautiful, if she does say so herself. She has been working on it almost since Merle left. Bunny frowns, digs the point of the scissors into her fingers again. Her brain has that feeling where you think it's a puddle but instead you slip on ice. She takes her jacket off and hangs it carefully over a hook on the back of the door. She takes her jeans off too, and holds the cuffs under the hot-air blower and after a while they feel dry and she puts them back on again.

It is hard to fall asleep. Bunny sits with her back against the wall, her legs stretched out in front of her, her feet braced against the pedestal of the sink. If only she had a cigarette. She gets up to drink from the sink again; the water is wavy like a little piece of string. Then she uses the toilet and feels better. She digs around in her knapsack, hoping she'd stuck her toothbrush and toothpaste in by accident and finds a lighter she didn't know she had. So she sits up for a while, flicking the lighter on and off, watching the shadows on the bathroom walls. Whenever she hears a rustling noise she flicks the lighter on. But it is just the wind outside blowing leaves against the door. Bunny gets up again to make sure the door is locked. Tomorrow she will find a drugstore and buy a toothbrush and toothpaste and some gum. She wonders what they said when they saw the mess. She wonders if her mother called the police.

Mook is such a jerk. He acts like the king of the world. Anytime she might be watching her favorite show he will switch to the ball game as if she weren't even there first. "Hey, I was watching something," she had protested the other night and he'd said, "Put a lid on it, Bunny," without even looking at her. She'd wanted to get up off the couch and go to her room but she'd have had to walk right past him. Then her mother had come in the room and had sat on Mook's lap. Bunny hated it when she did things like that. Couldn't she act more private?

Bunny holds the lighter on for a while until it begins to flicker. Just before she turns it out something catches her eye under the sink, a silvery button. She reaches for it, then puts it deep in the pocket of her jeans. Maybe this means Merlie is waiting for her. It is very exciting to have this thought and for a while it is even harder to fall asleep. Maybe Merle has left a trail of bread crumbs for Bunny to follow. She has to keep her eyes open for any sign.

2

THERE IS NO window in the bathroom but sunlight slides under the door. Bunny is so hungry when she wakes up that she eats a whole brownie. She knows it is a terrible idea, but maybe a whole brownie is better than a half.

Maybe a whole brownie will plow through her bad thoughts and come out the other side like a truck zooming through a paper sign. Anyway, there isn't anything else. She'll get the munchies but she has plenty of money to buy food when she gets somewhere. She wonders where the nearest town is. If she starts to freak she will just dig the scissors into her palm until it passes. She scratched her initials into her forearm last month. It didn't even hurt. In fact it felt good. She opens the bathroom door and sees it is a pretty day although she doesn't know what time it is. She closes the door fast. A man is striding toward the bathroom. She checks her image in the mirror.

Bang bang bang. A man is pounding on the door and hollering, "Get the hell out of there! Who's in there!"

"Nobody," says Bunny. She pushes her hair back from her face and refastens the barrette. She rinses her mouth quickly to make sure there's no chocolate on her teeth. Yelling makes her nervous. She has to get calm.

"Where's your car at," the man continues, still yelling, as if he hasn't heard Bunny at all. "I don't see no vehicle. This restroom is for patrons only. Just like a restaurant. I won't have no no-good punks living it up in there. Now you get on out before I call the police. I reckon you've had plenty of time to do whatever you're doing. Now get out!" *Bang bang.*

Bunny opens the door half an inch. There are big circles under her eyes from the mascara but she left them there because they look sophisticated. "I got a flat tire," she says.

"What are you doing in there?" asks the man, his voice softer. "You got a flat?"

Bunny nods, wipes a strand of hair out of the corner of her mouth.

"Where's your vehicle?" The man is squinting at her.

"It's a bike."

"Talk to me," says the man. He is wearing a blue shirt and the name over his pocket says *Earl*. Bunny has opened the door another inch. "Maybe I can give you a hand. Where's your bike at?"

"In the woods," says Bunny.

"Stop by the office," says the man. "I'll see what I can do for you."

"Okay," says Bunny. "You got any cigarettes?"

Earl shakes his head in disbelief and reaches into his shirt pocket. He pulls out a pack of cigarettes and shakes four into his hand, gives them to her. "You shouldn't smoke," he says. His fingers are warm and Bunny wishes he were her grandfather or something. She is always getting these wishes that come out of nowhere. "Oh, I know," says Bunny. "Neither should you."

The first drag always makes her want to puke, always makes her feel anxious; in fact, the whole first cigarette makes her feels sick and horrible. That is why she smokes it as fast as she can to get to the second, which is never as bad. Then by the third it doesn't bother her at all. There is a technique to everything. Thank goodness she didn't use up all the fuel in her lighter last night. She remembers the button and reaches down in her jeans pocket. It is still there. She didn't dream it.

Bunny folds up her tarp and sticks it in her knapsack. Ditto her jacket. She puts her sneakers back on and they feel cool and nice. It's going to be pretty hot today—already the sun is scorching. She doesn't have to clean up because she didn't make a mess. She doesn't wipe her heart off the mirror; she draws an arrow going through it and the words *Thank You*. She writes it with her lipstick. Then she opens the door and steps outside. The man is in the office and he isn't looking her way. He is talking on the phone. She feels mean not saying good-bye because he was nice, but she needs to get going. There is a sign that says NEW HOPE 14 MILES.

AFTER SHE HAS been walking a while Bunny comes to three houses on the right side of the road. They look like three little turned off television sets, each with a big gray picture window in front. Right in front of the first one is a lot of stuff on the lawn, and the words GARAGE SALE TODAY are painted on cardboard and nailed to a tree. There

are a bunch of dirty kids on tricycles riding in a circle, jin-
gling their little bells. One of the kids yells, "Hey! Cus-
tomer!" and they all stop to look at her and then start
riding around again.

Bunny lights her last cigarette and she sucks in her
stomach. She glances at the lawn with what she hopes is
a sophisticated expression and something catches her eye,
which is—this is so wierd—a scarf just like Merle's, red
with white fringe on it. She walks over casually, as if she
isn't really interested. But her heart is pounding. She picks
it up and presses it to her face, wondering if it will smell
like her sister. Merle wore patchouli oil. You could smell it
a mile away.

"You want it?" A woman's voice. Bunny looks up and
sees someone standing on the cement steps of the porch.
An American flag hangs off a pole there, kind of tattered at
the bottom. "Two fifty." Bunny reaches into her pocket and
withdraws ten quarters.

"Okay," she says. She walks over to the porch and
climbs two sagging steps to hand the woman her money.

"What you going to do with it? It's July." The woman
narrows her eyes as if she could see right through Bunny's
skin into her brain. This makes Bunny's scalp tickle.

"Yeah," says Bunny. She rolls the scarf up neatly and
puts it in her knapsack. Then Bunny frowns again, and
that shiny blank comes into her head. Like somebody put

a steel plate in there and she can't think for a second. But it gets better. Bunny wishes Merlie would write, but of course you can never tell what a person might be busy doing and not find time.

"You interested in anything else?" asks the woman.

"I'm just looking." Bunny coughs and takes another drag of her cigarette. She touches an old-fashioned record player.

"You interested in music?" the woman asks.

"Kind of," says Bunny, feeling warm all of a sudden. "My sister is."

"Last year I sold a lot of dance shoes," says the woman. "All colors. Does your sister dance?"

"She used to," says Bunny.

"Is that the truth."

"How much for the bicycle?" asks Bunny. Something in the woman's voice makes her uneasy. She is standing next to an old blue Schwinn. It is rusty but the tires are strong and the seat looks okay. She experiments with the kick-stand. Now that she's standing so close she realizes the woman smells like syrup. Maybe Merle bought the shoes.

"Fifteen," says the woman, wiping the back of her stringy neck with a white handkerchief.

Bunny turns her back to the woman and carefully peels a ten and a five off Mook's neatly wrapped bundle of bills. She hands them to the woman.

The woman eyes Bunny's backpack. "You're not from around here, are you? You camping somewhere?"

"Not exactly," says Bunny, her stomach rumbling.

"Don't suppose anybody ever called it pretty around here." She looks at the woods and then back at Bunny. "You had breakfast? Hungry?"

Bunny grips the handlebars tightly. The woman has such a friendly look. The kids are still yelling in the front on the gravel driveway. There are a bunch of straggly begonias in pots on the porch railing. "No," says Bunny, "not really."

"Do you like flapjacks?"

"Well, yes." A small brown dog comes snooping around and sniffs Bunny's left sneaker. "Hi, boy," she says, reaching down to touch its ears.

"I got some nice batter inside. You come on in with me. Now don't you argue, I don't take no for an answer. You can ask any one of the kids out there." She points to the driveway. "Rennie!" she yells. "You get up on the porch now and be ready to make change." A tall blond boy separates himself from the swarm and lopes toward the porch. He doesn't do more than glance at Bunny. He has blond eyebrows even, Bunny notices. She follows the woman into the house.

The front room is dark and smells like wet dog fur. There are only two windows. There's a big television with a broken antenna made of coat hangers on top and an ice cream sandwich wrapper sitting in an ashtray. There is a sofa with a blanket thrown over and the carpet is brown shag. The walls don't have any pictures except a framed painting of a big ocean wave the color of a sliced cucumber. A stack of magazines sits on an old beat-up coffee table in front of the sofa, and there is a fake green leather recliner that seems to be stuck in the recline mode. The living room makes Bunny feel sad in the pit of her stomach.

The kitchen is yellow with bright blue woodwork. There are glass bottles on the windows with red liquid inside like maraschino cherry juice and several blue bottles shaped like old fashioned cars with tiny little beads of colored candy inside. There are a bunch of dandelions that have turned brown on the windowsill in a jelly glass. Very fancy white organdy curtains are tied back at the window over the sink. A couple of geraniums on the sill have bright red flowers blooming. The sink stands on four legs and the garbage is underneath, in a paper bag with grease spots. Bunny is afraid it will split open right then if she stares at it. There are boxes on the counters, and piles of clothes.

"Getting ready to move," says the woman. "That's how come the sale. You like bananas sliced in? We're going down to North Carolina. My daughter's got a place down there now. My husband died last winter. Sometimes I think he's right in the other room. I doze off in the chair and think, well, he's just in the other room and then I think where is he? Carl? I call and then I realize. It takes getting used to." As she talks the woman is oiling a skillet and pouring pancake batter in. It smells good.

"I know what you mean," begins Bunny hesitantly. She wants to ask who bought the shoes.

The woman has an ear cocked toward the screen door. "Rennie? Get some change from over to Tyson's." She turns back to Bunny. "Sorry, honey, what?" But Bunny isn't in the talking mood anymore.

"Now tell me the god's honest truth," says the woman, putting a blue dish down in front of Bunny, then a fork and knife. "You can't be more than fourteen years old, can you?"

Bunny clears her throat. She has rehearsed this line. "I look young for my age. I'm almost eighteen."

"Uh-huh. You don't mind if I don't believe a word of that, do you?" The woman smiles. Her bottom teeth are crooked.

"You can believe what you want," says Bunny firmly, "but I'm going to be eighteen next month." She wishes she had another cigarette to light up and blow smoke around. The boy Rennie comes into the kitchen.

"Somebody wants the washing machine," he says, and

glances at Bunny. "But she wants it for thirty-five. You go talk to her."

"Get this little miss the syrup out of the fridge, will you?" She pronounces it "suurup," not "sirup."

"Are you running away?" Rennie asks when his mother has left.

"No." The tablecloth is red and sticky. The pitcher of syrup sits on a white saucer.

Bunny takes another big bite of pancake.

"You want some coffee?" The boy has his hand on an aluminum coffee pot. "Cream and sugar?" He holds out a small pitcher and points to the sugar bowl.

"Yes, please," says Bunny. Bunny pours more syrup and takes another bite. She takes a mug from the boy's hand. From outside come the yells and laughter of children. One of the dogs starts barking again. The boy sits down in the chair next to Bunny and pours himself a cup of coffee. He is one big freckle, Bunny thinks. She touches her own pale cheek.

"She's going to ask you if you want to stay for lunch."

"Well," says Bunny, "that's very nice but I'm in a hurry."

"She thinks you're running away."

"Well, I'm not. I'm meeting my father in New Hope."

"New Hope? You're a ways from there."

"Well, of course, I know that."

"New Hope's over on the Delaware River. I went rafting

there one time. You get in inner tubes and the current takes you. Is that what you're going to do?" As he speaks, Rennie gets up and slides another pancake onto the spatula, slips it onto Bunny's plate. She has eaten three.

"I don't know," says Bunny, pouring on more syrup.

The screen door bangs and a little girl runs into the kitchen. She is wearing a torn red dress and her feet are in a pair of very dirty white sandals. Her hair has been pulled back into a ponytail tied with a soiled red ribbon. Her face is grubby, her eyes a very dark brown. She must have been eating a Popsicle because she has a big pink clown mouth around her own mouth. She is also wearing a pair of dangle-down rhinestone earrings. Around her neck is a necklace of pink candies on an elastic string.

"Who are you?" she asks Bunny, sidling over to stand next to her, putting the string of candies into her mouth and starting to chew thoughtfully.

"My name is Mary," says Bunny. "Who are you?"

"Nina. What are you doing here?"

"I'm on a trip," says Bunny.

"Do you have any brothers?" the child asks.

"I have a sister." Bunny takes a bite of pancake.

"Where is she?"

"She's older than I am."

"But where is she? With your momma?"

"She's traveling right now."

"Where?"

"I'm looking for her," says Bunny. "You ask a lot of questions."

Rennie brings a sausage over. "She's a pest. You're a pest, aren't you, Nina."

"He's not my real brother," says Nina, climbing into Bunny's lap. "His name is Rennie. I hate him."

"Nina," says Rennie, "you are a pest."

"Rennie ate my pie." She shifts her position on Bunny's lap and her hard little bones dig into Bunny's thighs.

"You gave it to me."

"I didn't mean for you to eat it." Nina's lower lip trembles.

"Don't give it away if you want it yourself."

Nina decides to change the subject. "We used to have some rabbits." Nina points to a wire cage Bunny can now see on the back porch.

"What happened to them," asks Bunny.

"We ate them." A big tear rolls down Nina's cheek. "We ate them and Grandma told me it was chicken."

"Nina. Don't tell all your business." Rennie's voice is stern. "There wasn't nothing left to eat just then. You want a sausage?" he asks Bunny, but she shakes her head vigorously.

So much talk is making Bunny nervous. Rennie keeps trying to heap more food onto her plate. What is going on? Why is he being so nice? She reaches her left hand down in her jeans and finds the button. Good. Still there.

"They took it for forty," says the woman, who comes back into the kitchen wiping the back of her neck again. "I feel the heat something terrible. No time to be cooking. But things can't always wait, can they now." She is stirring something on the stove, sprinkling salt into a big pot. "Did you eat up good?" she asks Bunny, smiling. "Your arms are like little sticks, aren't they, Rennie? You need some meat on those bones, I swear. Why don't you stay for lunch."

"Oh!" A little shriek escapes Bunny. There is a big cage on the back porch—why didn't she put two and two to- gether before? That was why all the kids had fallen silent when she'd walked past them. The garage sale was just a trick. They're going to stick her in the cage and fatten her up and then cook her in the pot.

Bunny puts her fork down. She can't swallow at all. She gets up and she takes her knapsack. "I'm just going to check something," she says in a hoarse voice, and Rennie and the woman look at her blankly. "I just need to take a quick look at something outside," she says, edging toward the door. There is another car pulled up and two very fat women are climbing out of it. One of them has her hair in curlers. They look at her curiously. Are they going to eat over? Bunny walks quickly to the bike. "I bought this," she says in a loud voice. "I bought this fair and square." Rennie comes running over and puts his hand on the handlebars. Bunny thinks she will die right then and there. Die and then get eaten.

"Watch the brakes downhill, Mary," he says, and slides something over her left wrist. A Mickey Mouse watch. "Here," he says. "You need to know what time it is." Bunny doesn't know what to say. "Okay," she manages to croak out, and she gets going, over the gravelly driveway and onto the narrow road, pedaling as fast as she can.

"Hey!" she hears the woman calling after her. "Hey! You want some sandwiches?"

BUNNY ONLY SAW her dad a couple of times but she liked him. Now and then she took his memory out and ironed it, so to speak, before putting it back in her brain. Bunny stored things in her mind this way, like a linen closet. He was sad and didn't say much. The last time was about nine years ago. They went to the swing set and he bought her two chocolate ice cream cones and mostly he kept shaking his head and saying he was sorry and Bunny kept saying, "Oh, that's okay, Daddy," the word "Daddy" strange and special in her mouth, and she was proud to use it but wondered what would happen next. She was glad nobody was around to hear her say "Daddy" because they might ask, Who does she think she is? But actually it was just him and her at the end of the block on a hot August day. The playground was pretty small and grass never grew there really and her feet kicked up little puffs of dusty dirt because by mistake he had picked out the wrong swing, the baby swing, but she was proud of him anyway and proud to be with him, her own daddy, and she fixed it so her legs went stiffly out in front of her. He pushed her, and his hands at her back—up in the middle, higher than her waist, careful—she can still feel them if she shuts her eyes.

"Oh, you stupid baby," says Bunny to herself now, because she is crying. "You big baby." The bicycle is weaving along the road and it doesn't have any gears and the brakes aren't so hot but at least it goes, and Bunny wipes her eyes with her left hand. It's the stupid brownie. You have to eat them more frequently or your body doesn't know how to respond and drags out all the stupid sad stuff. She should just throw them away right now. But she doesn't. She isn't going to eat any more of them but she isn't going to throw them away yet either. After a while Bunny walks off the road and into the woods. She is still crying. She stays there leaning against a tree until she stops. When she has finished, she wipes her face and goes back onto the road.

3

SHE FEELS OKAY now, riding a bike makes her feel okay, pedaling, and she knows nobody was going to eat her up. For a while she kept looking behind her to see if the fat ladies were giving chase, but she calmed down. She is glad she left fast, before she said anything embarrassing. A couple of old cars have gone by, leaving clouds of black smoke. Burning oil, thinks Bunny, trying to hold her breath. She passes a little house. There is laundry hanging on the line and while she is looking at the big sheets flapping she almost rides over an animal squashed on the road. It is horrible, flat as a pancake. There isn't any blood, just this flat thing with its tail curled like a question mark.

She needs to keep away from weird thoughts so she concentrates on counting to eight, then counting to eight again. Nothing will charge out of the woods at her, not if she maintains a steady rhythm with the pedals. Bears can probably sense something, like sharks in the ocean can pick up irregular movement. One two three four five six seven eight. The sky is darkening again. Somewhere in the distance Bunny hears thunder getting ready, like a giant clearing his throat. Though I walk through the valley of the shadow of death. She could really go for a handful of Chiclets. That was partly why she brought so many quarters, Chiclet machines. They were good for energy and for getting cheered up, so sweet and interesting in her mouth.

Anyway, there aren't any bears around here.

She passes a bunch of red trash, paper cups and hot dog wrappers. Somebody threw their stuff out of a car, how nasty. She rides over a paper cup just for fun. She loves her bike, she wishes she could make it rear up like a stallion on its hind legs. She is letting her bike weave big S's all over the road since there aren't any cars. WELCOME TO AUGSVILLE POP. 653 reads a sign on her left with three bullet holes through it. The road changes into a street, Augsville. Bunny slows down and drives straight. How small. A few little stores, and a post office. There is a luncheonette sort of place called Paul's with a green-and-white striped awning which looks friendly and old-fashioned. She stops there, leaning Old Paint (it is embarrassing, but she has named her bike) against a little tree out front. The sidewalk is cracked. It feels weird to be off the bike at first, as if she doesn't know how to walk on the earth, as if she is five miles high and her feet are down there, so far away she can barely feel them. A bell chimes when she opens the screen door. It smells nice inside, like ice-cream-scoop water and peppermint toothpaste. The worn wooden floor is so slanty that if Bunny dropped a marble it would roll to the back of the store. There are two aisles that go to the back, where she sees the cash register and a lunch counter, on the right.

"Hi there."

"Oh hi." Bunny looks over to see a woman behind the luncheonette counter. She's wearing a pink-and-white checked dress with white buttons. Above her pocket it says *June* in flowery red script. The soda fountain is green Formica with red stools and a mirror on the wall behind. You could sit here and stare at yourself while you sucked up a black and white.

"Haven't seen you around." June is wiping the counter.

"No," says Bunny. "I haven't been here before."

"Don't fall for the quarter."

"What?"

June points to a silvery circle on the floor. "The quarter. See it?" Bunny nods and starts to bend down. "No. You try to pick it up and then you get a shock."

"Hasn't worked in years, Junie," comes a man's voice from the back of the store. "You know that."

"Oh, well, I won't try anyway. I already have some quarters." Bunny jingles her pockets.

"Looking for anything special?" June speaks again. She is leaning on the counter now, her chin in her hands. Why does everybody ask questions?

"Not really. Is there, like, a makeup section?"

"Nothing fancy sweetheart, go past the depilatories. No. Yes. Now look to your left."

Bunny picks out an emerald green waterproof masa-cara. There is a rack of postcards next to the makeup and Bunny takes her time choosing one. Most of them are of fishermen catching fish, but there is one of a waterfall and Bunny buys that and a ballpoint pen. Bunny walks down another aisle past shaving cream and shampoo and stops in front of the toothpaste. "I don't know how I could have left my toothbrush back at my aunt's," she says moments later, laying everything out on the counter in the back of the store. Bunny smiles at the gray-haired man behind the cash register but he isn't looking at her, he is pricing the toothpaste. "Two packs of Marlboros please."

To Bunny's relief he rings up the cigarettes, no questions asked. He even throws in a book of matches. Bunny pays and thanks him and then she walks over and sits at the lunch counter. There is a man with a bunch of keys hanging off his belt sitting at the farthest over stool. He is leaning over his plate. His back is so broad, he reminds Bunny of Mook—god, he could be Mook's long-lost brother or something. June is filling his coffee cup. Bunny minds her own business and and takes out her postcard and new pen. "Dear Merle," she writes in very tiny print, "Wish you were here. I'll see you pretty soon I hope. Love,

Bunny." And then she makes up an address: "1314 Fountain Road, New Hope Pa." That is in case anybody is watching. She doesn't know Merle's address.

"What can I do you for?" June is standing in front of her now, holding her pad and pencil.

"Could I have a Coke please?" Bunny covers the postcard with her left hand.

"Anything to go with that? Cheeseburger, honey? BLT?"

"Oh, no thanks," says Bunny, sliding the card and the pen back into the paper bag. "Just a Coke." She is suddenly wondering if Merlie had come this way and sat here on this exact green stool and looked at this exact same worn spot on the counter. Bunny would like to think so, it makes her feel closer to Merle. Maybe some of Merle's molecules are still in the air, even. Bunny takes a deep breath. The waitress sets a Coke down in front of her. "Thank you," says Bunny.

"Don't mention it."

Bunny is thinking about Merle so hard that she is sure Merle was actually here. She wants to ask them if anybody remembers seeing her, but it was a while ago now. She wonders if Merle came in and maybe mentioned where she was headed. Bunny frowns. She always comes up against the ice here. She sticks her hand in the pocket and feels the button. It is soft and smooth in her hand. She should be looking for another sign, but so far there is nothing besides a hunch. She shivers a little, and digs into her knapsack to make sure her jacket is still there. The scarf. Her tarp. It has begun to rain.

"Bob's got his raffle again," says June, looking out the window. "Gonna ask us to buy a five-dollar ticket to a two-dollar show. What do I want with a free hairdo anyway. My sister owns the damn beauty parlor. I can get it for free anytime." June pats her short blond hair.

"Is that so," snickers the man five stools down eating a hamburger. Ketchup spurts out and Bunny thinks of Dracula. "Hey, Paulie. June says she can get it for free anytime. What do you say to that?" From somewhere in the back the other man laughs. "Tell me where, honey," he says. "Just tell me where."

"Can it," says June. She lights a cigarette and blows an enormous smoke ring that hovers in the air as big as a hubcap. Bunny can't take her eyes off it. While she's watching June blows another smaller ring right through the big one. "You meeting someone, honey?"

"Yes. At the corner over there," she says. "My father. We're from New York City," she adds, as if that explains everything.

"Tell you why I asked. Got a couple of doughnuts going begging. You take them with you. What's your name, sweetheart?"

"Honey," says Bunny. "I know it's a weird name, but

that's what my daddy wanted to call me the second I was born. 'Isn't she a honey,' those were his exact words."

"Sounds like you've got a fine daddy," said June, stubbing her cigarette out. "You tell him I said hi, will you?"

"Sure," says Bunny. "Sure I will."

"Because good daddies are few and far between," says June, raising her voice a little bit and glancing toward the back of the store. "Wouldn't you say that was right, Paul," she says.

"Relax," says the invisible Paul.

"You be sure and tell him honey, won't you?" June is wiping the counter again with a big rag. Slap slap. Although it is already clean.

"Oh yes, I will," says Bunny. She hesitates, but she likes June and she can feel Merle around her in this place. "You know, I think my sister might have passed through this way," says Bunny. "It was about a year ago? Maybe a little more than a year ago." Bunny ticks off months on her fingers, although she knows exactly how many months it has been. Fourteen.

"Not that many folks pass this way," says June.

"She's taller than me and much more, you know, filled out, and she has hair that goes all the way down her back."

"I don't recall. Fourteen months is a long time even in this sleepy little bugtown, sweetheart. Where is she now?"

"Really red hair." Bunny says. Bunny looks into the mirror now and sees a shadowy shape. Bunny holds her breath and doesn't move, waiting for Merle to say something, afraid to turn around. Her heart is beating and beating. Outside it is thundering and lightning again. *Merle, is that you Merle?*

"There was the terrible thing a while back." The hamburger man is talking with his mouth full. "Over by New Hope, wasn't it? That girl they found strangled? Terrible."

"You okay, sweetheart?" asks the waitress, whose cool hand is by now covering Bunny's own. "You look a little woozy there. We don't allow fainting in here, do we, Paul."

"I'm okay. Got to go now." The shape is gone.

June protests but Bunny is already halfway to the door. She is mad at herself. She can usually tell when somebody is going to say something she doesn't want to hear. But she didn't see it coming.

Outside it is raining hard, like little eggs coming down, splashing.

YOU LEAVE TRACES of yourself, Bunny thinks, everywhere you've been. Silvery shapes. She has thought hard about it, because to tell the truth this isn't the only time she has seen Merle. The first time was on the bus that goes up Broadway. Bunny had been outside the Cathedral Market. There in the third window, her face against the glass, was

Merle. She hadn't smiled, she hadn't waved, she had just fixed her eyes on Bunny. She'd looked sad. Bunny had run after the bus shouting and waving, but it hadn't stopped. She misses me, Bunny says to herself, she'll send me a sign. Bunny just has to be in the right place at the right time and presto, there will be Merle. Maybe Merle has opened an embroidery business in New Hope, with a changed name. Maybe Bunny will walk across a little green bridge and find her there, maybe her hair cut short, maybe dyed black. Anything can happen.

4

THE AUGSVILLE SUD-Z Laundromat is set back off the street, with a parking lot out front. Bunny is sitting on a bench against the back wall pretending to be doing a crossword puzzle while pretending to be waiting for wash. Outside it is raining cats and dogs. There were a few people here when she first came in but nobody noticed Bunny. Everybody was busy folding. Except one boy who was stuffing a sopping wet blanket into a dryer. It dripped on the floor and nobody said anything. Then he left.

Bunny can see the blanket going around in the dryer, probably still wet. Everyone is gone now except one mother and her baby. The mother's mouth looks like a dent in her face, and her hair is separated into greasy strands and her arms are fat but she is wearing a sleeveless shirt and too tight shorts. The baby is skinny. The woman is trying to get stuff out of the dryer and into one of those big carts but the baby cradled in her left arm keeps crying. It sounds as if it can't get enough air to scream, so it just quacks like a duck. Finally the woman sighs, holds the baby with both arms, and goes to stand at the back door, which is propped open by a chair. Bunny watches her patting the baby's back. Beyond the door Bunny can see a rusted metal picnic table and a couple of plastic chairs. Rain falling all over everything. After a while the child quiets down. Bunny looks at her watch. It is only two-thirty. Bunny hates two-thirty. What a nothing time.

Bunny isn't sure what to do next. She is waiting for a sign. The crossword puzzle was lying on the bench when she came in and she hoped it had a message for her. But all of the questions are about golf. One of the filled-in blanks says IGOR and another NED. All the rest of them say ROLAND. *Roland* can't be the answer to everything, and besides the name is squeezed in when there are only three spaces. But who knows. Bunny doesn't do crosswords. That was Merle's specialty. "What's a four-letter word for *asshole*," Merle whispered to Bunny once. "Mook," was the answer, and Bunny had giggled until she'd almost peed her pants. That was a couple of years ago, when everything was okay. Now the world is enormous, full of small black roads that hardly go anywhere. She wishes she could take a hot shower. She thinks about the bathroom back home, with Mook's razor and toothbrush. "Mook likes his coffee with milk in the A.M." her mother had said, as if Bunny gave a good goddamn. She'd like to serve him up a nice hot cup of dog piss and see how he liked that.

"You want a tissue?"A soft voice startles Bunny. She realizes she is sitting forward on the bench with her shoulders hunched up and her hands under her thighs and is just staring at nothing whatsoever in the shape of a washing machine. She touches her face, which is wet as if she has been crying. The crossword has slid to the floor.

"I've got a diaper you can use." The fat mother is holding a cloth out to her. Bunny sees she is young.

"Thanks," says Bunny, wiping her eyes.

"You can keep it," says the mother. "I've got plenty more." She is piling things into a yellow laundry cart and pushing them over to the table in back for folding. The baby is asleep.

"What a cute baby," says Bunny, to be polite.

"Looks like his old man. Bald as a bat." The woman smiles a little. Still, her mouth is kind of caved in. Bunny watches her fold the diapers expertly, she watches her fold up the tiny baby clothes and a couple of crib sheets. She folds up some large underpants and a tremendous pair of shorts, bright red. She is just going along as if everything were normal and yet she is so terrible looking.

"Want some help?" Bunny asks.

"I got it, thanks," the woman replies, her chin holding one end of a towel to her chest, managing to fold it up neatly with her left hand while her right arm holds the sleeping baby. "You get good at this." She smiles again. She doesn't have any top teeth, that's what's the matter.

Five minutes later the woman is ready to leave, everything folded and put in a green laundry basket. "Bye-bye," she says.

"Oh, bye-bye." Bunny waves to them, the baby asleep on his mother's shoulder.

She feels a little weird now that she has the whole place to herself. Only one washing machine still going and as Bunny sits listening to it spin, it stops. There isn't any noise at all now except the fan and the dryer with the blanket. She doesn't want to just sit here but she doesn't know exactly what to do and she is tired of her boring mind, which has nothing in it she wants to think about. She digs around in the knapsack and unearths the foil-wrapped brownie. She looks to make sure nobody is watching her through the window, then she breaks off a big piece and pops it into her mouth. It tastes so weird, kind of like mud. Now she lights a cigarette. Chocolate makes you want to smoke. Maybe she should throw a few things into a washer. Her sneakers, for instance. They're starting to smell bad and her feet feel slimy. She gets up and buys some packets of soap from a machine on the wall. Just for fun and because she has so many quarters she drops one sneaker in one washer and the other sneaker in another. She wishes she could wash her clothes but she has nothing to change into. There is nothing in her knapsack to wear except her jacket, unless you count the tarp. At least it's summer and she doesn't need much. And the linoleum feels cool under her bare feet. Now she is thinking about Merle's flip-flops. They were the color of red peppers or paprika or those teeny tiny red spiders that you sometimes see, but they weren't meant for running. The last time Bunny saw Merle she was running. "Go home, Bunny," she had yelled, as if she were angry with Bunny. "Don't follow me now."

"But your shoes!" Bunny had held one up.

Merle hadn't turned around again. Fourteen months ago Merle crossed the street barefoot and turned the corner down Broadway.

Suddenly Bunny feels bad for her sneakers. They must feel so all alone tumbling around in the great big machines with no other company. She walks over to the big table against the wall where all the lost-and-found stuff is. There are a lot of socks. She throws a couple of socks in with one sneaker, a couple more with the other. Company. Then she goes back to the table and picks one-handed through the pile, holding her cigarette off to the side. Maybe there is something here she could wear while she washed and dried her clothes. Bunny pauses, the cigarette in her right hand, a graying Dacron blouse in her left. Sometimes sad clothes space her right out. She drops it back on the table. She picks up a Mickey Mouse T-shirt with a huge stain on the front. Maybe she could wear that, it comes down to her knees. She stands there picking off the pinkish gray lint. Then quickly she pulls the big T-shirt over her head like a tent and slips out of her jeans. She pulls on a pair of purplish lost-and-found slacks, which fit okay, a little big. Then she throws her clothes into a third washer (good thing she brought so many quarters) and sits back down on the bench, the crossword puzzle in her lap. She feels a little strange sitting in somebody else's clothes. What if they come in and demand them back? She wishes Merle would show up soon, or at least send her some message. Her cigarette is burned down to the filter, balanced on the edge of the lost-and-found table, where she left it.

In the bottom of her knapsack is one postcard from Merle. It is dated almost fourteen months ago to the day. Bunny almost never looks at the postcard because it is already so worn and wrinkled from when she used to look at it all the time. Now she keeps it wrapped in tin foil and sealed in a Baggie. She thinks about looking at it now. But why? She already knows what it says. It's just she likes to touch the ink. The postmark was New Hope.

Merle ran away on a Saturday morning. Bunny was already up and eating toast and jelly in the kitchen. Momma was in a bad mood because there wasn't any milk for Mook's coffee. Merle had come into the kitchen wearing a pair of cutoffs and a boob tube and Momma had looked at her and her mouth had gone tight and her eyes had gotten little. She tried to stare Merle down. Merle opened the icebox and looked for the milk. "Out of milk?" she asked casually. She must have just come out of the shower because her hair was wet and hung down her back, starting to go curly the way it always did when it dried. Momma's hair was like Bunny's, kind of boring, although she gave herself permanents.

"And I wonder who drank it up," said Momma, banging her glass down on the table.

"Wasn't me, don't look at me." said Merle. "Mook's the one drinks the milk around here." Merle was cracking eggs into a bowl.

"He didn't touch the milk."

Merle opened the drawer and took out a fork. "Want some French toast, Bunzie?" Merle asked.

"She's eating already," snapped their mother.

"Take it easy, Mom," said Merle, "Don't get your knickers in a twist." She turned her back to her mother and a big patch of bare skin showed through the ass of her shorts.

That was all Momma could stand and she started yelling tramp this and tramp that, and what did she think she was doing wearing clothes like that. Bunny stared immediately at her toast. The jelly made purple mountains majesties on her toast. Above the fruited plain. Bunny hated fights. Momma kept yelling and the louder Momma screamed the softer Merle answered, which drove Momma crazy. "I'm an expert at Mother," Merle liked to say. "Watch her turn bright red and sputter like a goddamn firework." But she said it without smiling.

"I know what you're doing," Momma began to scream. "You're coming on to Mook!" Bunny picked up the last of her toast and went into the living room.

"Mook? Coming on to Mook? In his dreams!" Merle started to laugh.

Bunny heard a crash, and then a yell. She ran back to the kitchen. The bowl of eggs was knocked to the floor and Merle had a handprint across her cheek. "Look what she's holding! She's threatening me!" yelled Momma, pointing at Merle. Merle had the fork in her hand.

"You hit me," said Merle evenly. "Don't hit me again." And then Mook came lumbering down the hall.

"What the hell is this?" He stood in the doorway in his

undershirt and shorts. He stared at Merle, who still held the fork. "What the hell is going on?" he asked.

"She's threatening me," Mother said, grabbing Mook's big arm and pointing to Merle. Merle looked from Momma to Mook and back again.

"I didn't touch you," she said to Momma.

"Look at the way she's holding that fork! Just look at the look on her face!" Momma was beginning to scream again. "I want to call the cops. Call the cops, Mook. I want her out of here. I want her in custody." Mook moved toward Merle.

"Is that what you want, Merle?" Mook took a step forward.

Merle rolled her eyes but her chin was trembling. Then she put the fork on the counter. "I'm out of here," she said, taking her jacket off the back of the chair. "I'm history. I'm smoke."

"What did I tell you," screamed Momma.

"Where are you going?" Bunny asked when Merle brushed past. Momma began screaming again and Mook yelled at Merle to stop right there or not bother coming back. "Wait up! Merle!" Bunny started down the stairs after her. She heard Mook saying, "Girl is out of control," just before her momma slammed the door. But it had looked to Bunny like Merle was crying. Even from the back Bunny was sure Merle was crying, only Merle never cried. Bunny felt very strange. Everything was wrong.

"Don't follow me, Bunny!" Merle had yelled, the only time she had ever raised her voice to Bunny, and Bunny had stopped on the sidewalk. Dead in her tracks.

ONE TWO THREE four five six seven eight. Nine washing machines. Five dryers and three really big dryers. A bulletin board with six red thumbtacks and eleven white ones. Counting things works when she feels weird. She makes herself go out front and buy an RC cola, the nice tumbling sound of the can coming from somewhere deep inside and winding up in the little bin down below, frosty and cold. The sneaker machines are done and Bunny fishes them out along with the socks. She throws them in the same dryer. *Wham clunkity boom boom boom.* Sneakers make a lot of noise. The dryer with the big blanket has stopped. Bunny opens it and touches the blanket, which is still damp. Out of kindness she puts in three more quarters and the blanket starts up again, whirling and plopping, whirling and plopping.

Bunny sits on the bench and puts her head between her knees and her hands over her ears. She is getting the tiny dot feeling. This is where Bunny suddenly feels like a tiny dot in the middle of everything so big and her only this tiny dot. It makes her need to not move. She has gotten used to the slippery ice feeling, but not the tiny dot feeling. It is worse. She would like to make herself walk around and look at things but it is dangerous to get off the chair. She doesn't make a sound either, once she tried talking but it was like her voice was coming from a corner of the ceiling, far away. That was terrible, because she knew she was going crazy. In her mind she says, Though I walk through the valley of the shadow of death, but it doesn't work, the words just fall away from her like scraps.

IT IS GETTING dark now and Bunny is still in the Laundromat. At the moment she is holed up in the utility closet, which contains a big metal bucket with a wringer and a mop and a couple of bags of maybe lint or something, she isn't sure. Her forehead feels hot and her arms feel shaky. She should never have gotten herself in the hiding mood because it is so hard to get out of it. She hopes nobody will want to use anything in here. She is wrapped in the boy's blanket (which he never came back for and she figures is now partly hers) and she must have been asleep because her watch says seven-thirty. It glows in the dark. She pictures herself in a little gray tepee. In her lap she's got her knapsack and the crossword puzzle book. For a while she was just giggling in here, but that stopped and she fell asleep. You can't always tell what kind of mood you'll be in. There's no way to exactly regulate the amount of brownie that works to make you feel sleepy and good.

She has heard people come and go. Sometimes their footsteps come right next to the closet door like when they stand by the soap machine. "Where is your sister!" she imagines somebody pushing the door open and shouting. Now she hears dryers banging open and closed one after another. Somebody is out there. She gets way under the blanket and curls up as small as she can. If only there were coats she could hide behind. Somebody is standing right outside the closet door. Did she leave a trail? Is she, like, phosphorescent? The next thing she knows the door is being pulled open.

"What the hell is this?" A boy's voice. "That's mine," he says, pulling the blanket off her head. Bunny's hair is all staticky and she can't see because the light is so bright with the door open.

"I didn't know it was yours." Bunny's voice sounds rusty.

"I left that sucker in a dryer." He is staring at her. "What are you doing in the closet?"

"You don't have to yell." She shades her eyes to look at him but she has to squint because the light is so bright behind him. She doesn't know what else to say and neither of them speak.

"I don't appreciate thieves." He holds the blanket up now, inspecting it for damage. As if Bunny might have chewed holes in it like a moth or a dog. Then he looks more carefully at her. She is still sitting on the floor. "Well, no hard feelings." As he speaks he begins to fold the blanket into smaller and smaller squares.

Bunny wishes she had put on her mascara. She had had all the time in the world to fix her face and instead she fell asleep. She tries to brush the hair out of her eyes but it is still full of static from the blanket. Everything tickles and both her feet are asleep. She can't even stand up yet. It is so embarrassing.

"You been here long?" He has curly hair and his face gets twisted when he smiles. Her eyes are adjusting.

"I was on a trip with my father but I got lost," she says.

"Uh-huh." He looks about fifteen. He is tall and kind of skinny with a red shirt on and jeans.

"Where is Augsville," she asks after a silence. "I mean, like, what is it near that I've heard of."

"Depends what you've heard of. We're a long way from gay Paree."

"I mean which side of the river is it on."

"That depends on the river."

"The Hudson?"

"We're west of the Hudson. Fifty, sixty miles."

"The Delaware?"

"We're east of the Delaware. Couple miles. Where are you headed?"

"I was on my way to New Hope. My dad and I are meeting people there and possibly my sister."

"Where's your dad?"

"We were supposed to meet there. My bike is outside."

"What's your name?"

"Bunny."

"What's your real name."

"That is my real name. Bunny."

"My name is Roland." He reaches down to shake hands. "I was just washing my sneakers." His hand is very warm.

"Roland?" A woman's voice. Bunny shrinks back against the wall.

"Hey. June-bug." Roland pushes the closet door partly shut with his foot.

"You seen anybody belongs to this bike?"

"Blue bike out there?"

"Yeah. You seen anybody?" June's voice doesn't sound like it's coming closer.

"Like who. I've seen lots of anybodys today."

"No need to get smart, Roland. You see a girl maybe fourteen, fifteen you give me a call, will you? Brown hair, not much meat on her. Jeans. A big green knapsack stuffed with god knows what. You hear?"

"Rob a bank?"

"Runaway. I thought she'd taken off but maybe she's still around somewhere. Nobody in here when you came in tonight?"

"Do you see anybody?" He shrugs. "Place looks empty to me."

Bunny eyes are shut tight. She hates questions. She hates it when people are too nice.

"She had some cock-and-bull story about her daddy meeting her later. But she keeps worrying my mind. If you see her, give me a call. She might need a place to stay."

"Sure thing."

"Just call down to the store. Roland? You still got that dog, for cripes' sakes?"

"Dog's got me, what can I tell you."

"Put it to sleep, Roland. Take my advice. No life for a dog." Bunny hears the door bang shut.

He opens the closet door. "You running away?"

"Of course not," says Bunny. She is trying to stand up but her feet are to the ticklish part where it feels like they're made out of electric hairbrushes.

"Listen, Bunny," says Roland. "They shut this place in half an hour. You want a place to sleep tonight? Bunny?" Roland's hand is on her arm. She wonders if he can tell what she is thinking. She is thinking, could she stab him with her tiny scissor if she had to? She hates what her mind thinks. She needs to sit still and hold her head in her hands. Otherwise she might go crazy in some different new way. Her thoughts are tiny airplanes crashing into each other in the big space inside her head. *Whirr whirr crash plop.* Now they are lying on little cots with the covers up to their chins. They are in the thought hospital. Some of them move their feet under the sheets but they are pale as ghosts or the white part of bacon.

"Bunny?" He keeps interrupting her. "I know a place you can crash for the night."

Crash. Bunny almost giggles.

"Are you okay?"

No answer from Bunny. She needs to hold her head still in her hands.

"Hey! What's the matter?" Roland is leaning down so close she can feel his breath. "Is something wrong? You feel sick?"

She shakes her head. "I'll be okay." Her voice sounds husky and she still has her face hidden in her hands. "Sometimes I get a little weirded out."

"Hey. Don't we all. Listen. They're closing the Laundromat soon."

"My feet are asleep," she says. "I can't walk right."

Bunny gets to her feet with Roland's help and they slip out the back.

5

"WHERE'S YOUR FOLKS?" asks Bunny. They are standing in a tiny kitchen. The sink is filled with dishes and a pot on the stove is crusty with old chili. "Do you live here all by yourself?"

"My dad totaled himself," says Roland casually, making the motion of tipping a bottle to his lips and drinking.

"Oh. I'm sorry."

"That's okay. Don't worry about it. Happened years ago."

"Where's your mom?"

"And my mom is away. I always clean up just before she gets back and I don't sleep in the house until she comes home. I sleep in the car."

"What kind of car?"

"It's a seventy-five Chevy station wagon. It's out back. It's an antique."

A station wagon. Bunny was just thinking about station wagons the other day. Maybe this is a sign that she is on the right track.

Roland is still talking. "My dog lives in the car. My mom isn't a dog person really."

"Is she coming back tonight?" Bunny picks up the lid of a brown teapot and puts it back. The tea inside has a green bubble floating on it.

"She had a little breakdown. She's pretty highly strung. But I'm old enough to take care of myself." Roland frowns. He is opening and closing cupboard doors.

"Did she ever feel tiny? Like a dot?"

Roland tosses her a bag of potato chips. His eyes are really brown. "I don't know. When she gets that way she doesn't talk. You hungry?" Roland now opens the fridge. "When she comes home she only eats graham crackers and milk," he says. "So we can't eat those. Hey. I know. How about sour-cream-and-onion-soup dip? I've got a lot of that. Yeah. Here it is." He brings out a container.

"I love onion dip," says Bunny.

"Then we'll just grab those chips and head out to the car. You want to grab a couple of Cokes from the fridge?" He turns out the lights. "You done in here?"

It is getting dark. Cricket sounds are everywhere. There are the lights from another house through the trees. They descend the three sagging porch steps and go out to the garage in the back. There is the station wagon. It is dark green with fake wood. Roland opens the front door and Bunny looks inside. There is a small dog on the seat.

"What's his name?"

Roland goes around to the other side and slips into the driver's seat. "Buster."

Roland's right hand is resting gently on the dog's head. Bunny can see now that it's only with great effort that the dog is sitting up. He keeps trembling and sliding back to lying down. One hind leg shakes and shakes. "Poor thing," she says.

"He's okay. He's just under the weather, that's all."

"His nose is awfully dry," says Bunny, reaching out a hand. "Isn't that a sign that he's sick?" But Roland doesn't seem to have heard her. "Maybe he should drink a little water."

"He won't drink. I don't think he's thirsty. I don't like to bother him too much, you know? He just likes to lay his head on my lap like this and rest. Good dog." Roland smooths the hair on his head, and runs his hand gently down the dog's flank. The dog shivers with pleasure. He sits down on the seat next to Buster, moving the animal very carefully onto his lap.

"I think maybe he should go to the vet."

"I already did that." Roland looks down at Buster. "Hey Buster, who's my boy, huh, who's my best dog, Buster. See that?" Bunny sees the dog's tail wag slightly. "Climb in the back. You can stretch out and there's a pillow too." Bunny settles herself, putting her knapsack on the floor of the car. Roland is fussing with something in Buster's ear. "Shit," he says softly. "Is that a goddamn tick? How'd you get a tick, Buster?" His voice is so gentle.

"You should use tweezers. You could get sick from

ticks. I had one in my ear once. My sister took it out with tweezers." Bunnny opens the sack of potato chips.

"Your sister isn't here and neither are her tweezers. Hold still, boy." Roland's hands are nice and calm. Bunny watches him carefully feeling around the dog's ear.

"Oh. She ran away one time and she hasn't come back yet. She can't write because then my mother would know where she is. She could have her traced by the postmark." Bunny talks with her mouth full.

Roland doesn't say anything. He takes a flashlight out of the glove compartment. It has gotten dark. "No kidding," he finally says.

"She wants me to know where she is but she doesn't dare write. I only got one postcard. She and my mother got in these tremendous fights and she got sick of it. She needs to live her own life." Another three potato chips disappear into Bunny's mouth. She is so hungry and these are so salty and good.

Roland is shining the light in the animal's ear. "It's nothing. Good dog." He looks back at her. "When did she leave?"

"Oh, a couple of months ago I think. A year. Maybe a little longer." Bunny leans against the pillow. The seat is very soft.

Roland puts the flashlight back in the glove compartment. "That's plenty of time to get her shit together."

"Uh-huh."

"Maybe something happened to her."

"No. She sends me messages."

"Messages? You mean she calls you up?"

"Oh no, nothing like that. My mother could trace the call. She leaves me clues. I found a button, for instance. And a scarf."

"Like a scavenger hunt?" Something in his voice sounds like a joke and Bunny doesn't feel like talking anymore.

"It isn't funny."

"What did the postcard say."

"You wouldn't understand. It was in code."

"Try me."

Bunny shakes her head. "It's private."

"Why are you suddenly looking for her now?"

"I don't know," says Bunny. "I guess I didn't know I could before."

"What did you say your sister's name was?"

But suddenly Bunny doesn't want to tell.

"Honey," she says. "Honey-Lou Simmons."

"Never heard of her," says Roland. "Pass me some chips." He passes the container of dip over the backseat. Bunny makes a little pile of potato chips in her lap and takes the dip. They eat for a while, passing the dip back and forth over the seat. She snaps open a Coke and hands the other to Roland.

"Thank you very much," she says shyly. "This is so good."

"Buster usually likes this too but he isn't hungry tonight. Are you, Buster."

They are both quiet. The dog sighs.

"Do you know how to get there? To New Hope?" Bunny asks after a silence.

"You get on the River Road and you pedal like crazy."

"Where is the River Road?"

"Not so far," says Roland. "Maybe I'll show you myself tomorrow. Right now it's time for some shut-eye. Scared of the dark?"

"Not too much."

"Personally, I like the dark."

"I don't mind it either."

"Hey. Horse walks into a bar."

"What?"

"Horse walks into a bar. Bartender asks, 'Why the long face?'" Roland starts to laugh. "That cracks me up every time. 'Why the long face?'"

"I don't get it."

"Nothing to get. That's the beauty of it. A horse has a long face. He can't help it."

"Oh."

"Never mind. If you get cold there's a blanket back there."

Bunny curls up under the big gray blanket. Cricket sounds are everywhere.

"I'm sorry about your dad," whispers Bunny, but Roland doesn't answer.

Once Merle had kissed Bunny right on the lips. Bunny was missing her dad really bad, even though she hadn't seen him since she was, like, four, she could still remember him and sometimes it made her so sad and nobody knew where he was either, and Bunny pictured him all alone and begging with a cup somewhere and nobody even looking at him and rain coming down and she began to cry and Merle said, "What's the trouble, bubble?" and Bunny said, "I miss my daddy" and Merle had gotten such a funny look and she had held Bunny's chin in her hand and tipped her face up and bent down and kissed her directly right on her mouth. Bunny had thought Merle's lips tasted like the softest thing she'd ever felt, nothing in the world was as soft as Merle's lips, no wonder boys went crazy for her, and she hadn't known what to do or say after. She had stopped crying and wiped her face and then they had gone downtown for pizza.

6

WHEN BUNNY WAKES up and looks at her watch it is seven-thirty. It is so quiet except for the woods sounds that she thinks at first Roland must still be asleep, lying down in the front. She peeks over the front and he is gone—only the dog is there, lying still. She watches very carefully until she can discern the faint rise and fall of breath by his rib cage. "Poor doggie," she whispers. There is a note on the dashboard. "Back soon. Gone to get supplies." She rubs her eyes and opens the car door, closing it behind her softly so as not to scare the dog. She takes her knapsack and goes into the house to use the bathroom. There is tooth powder, not toothpaste, on the sink and the bottom of the can has left a couple of rusty ovals. On a shelf above the sink is a bottle of Cornhusker's Lotion and Bunny tries to take the top off to sniff but it is rusted shut. She looks in the mirror and smiles. Her teeth aren't yellow yet. She combs her hair with her fingers. She washes her face and dries it with her T-shirt as there aren't any towels in the bathroom except one that she thinks might have once been used for the dog. There isn't even any toilet paper in the bathroom but instead a box of torn-up magazines and newspapers.

As she is brushing her teeth such a terrible thought comes into her head. What if Merle has been living all this time in New Hope? What if she is living there happily and didn't want to send for Bunny? What if she never even thinks about Bunny at all and doesn't care if she ever sees Bunny again? This is such a terrible thought that Bunny has to sit down on the edge of the tub and empty her knapsack. There at the bottom, under the scarf and the tarp and her embroidered jacket is the little thin package containing the postcard. She takes it out, unwrapping its many layers.

Dear Bunzie,
It's beautiful. Wish you were here.
XO Merle.

Bunny's fingers touch the writing and she presses her face against it. Then she turns it over. The front of the card is a green bridge over a blue river and a ballpoint *X* in the sky with an arrow pointing down to the middle of the bridge. "X marks the spot," it says in Merle's tiniest handwriting, "where I'm writing this." The postmark was New Hope. Bunny holds the card against her ear as if it might whisper something to her.

"Breakfast," says Roland, knocking on the bathroom door, startling Bunny. Hastily she puts the card back in her knapsack. "I hope you take cream and sugar because I put it in both," he calls through the door.

"Oh, thank you," says Bunny, "but I don't eat breakfast."

"You need something in your stomach if you're going to New Hope. It's a nice day today, perfect day for a bike ride."

When Bunny comes into the kitchen he points proudly out the window. There in the backyard are two bikes, one green, one red. The green one has a big basket on the handlebars. Neither of them is Old Paint, but she doesn't want to say anything. They left too fast last night to bring her own bike.

"Whose are those? " she asks.

"Mine." He nods. "I'm going to take you. Buster's coming too, in the basket. He's a water dog, lots of spaniel in him, and I think the river will do him good."

"I didn't think he looked too good this morning," says Bunny. "There's some foam coming out of his mouth."

"I think I know my own dog," says Roland and his tone is so sharp. She takes a big swallow of coffee.

"Here. Eat something." He holds the bag of doughnuts out. Maybe he noticed that she got her feelings hurt. "Go on. They've got little jimmies on them. Coconut too. Don't tell me you can resist a chocolate coconut doughnut."

Bunny shakes her head.

"So are you ready to go?" he asks. "Destination New Hope?"

Bunny shrugs.

"Well, what are we waiting for?" He picks up the blanket and carries it out to the bike, where he folds it into the basket. Then he brings the dog out of the car and places him gently on top, handling him as if he were made of liquid. Bunny watches from the back steps as if this were her house and Roland were leaving. She is eating a doughnut now. "So saddle up, Bunny," says Roland, beckoning and smiling. "We can be there in half an hour. We'll buy some sandwiches and have a picnic. Come on. You'll love it." He throws one leg over the seat. Bunny hesitates. It's like she is made of Jell-O, or holes or something. She can't seem to get any energy all of a sudden. She didn't know it was so close. Half an hour.

"Wait."

"What for? You're not ready?"

"I forgot my knapsack." And she goes into the kitchen and comes out with it over her shoulders. But still she hesitates.

"Let's go," Roland drums his fingers on the handlebars.

"I don't know."

"You don't know what?"

"Maybe today isn't the right day," she says.

"What's wrong with today? It might rain again tomorrow. Today is perfect. Look at that sky," he says, pointing into the air.

"Let me think a second."

"What's the matter?" asks Roland. "You don't want to go? I thought that was what you wanted to do."

"I know. Okay. It is. Okay." She stands there straddling the bike.

"So let's get this show on the road." Roland starts off down the driveway toward the street and Bunny follows.

"Let's not go too fast," she says.

They are on the road now, pedaling along, Roland talking to the dog in his basket and Bunny riding behind. But the ride is so short. In hardly any time they are almost there.

"Hey," says Roland. "Steep hill coming up. New Hope in sight practically."

Bunny wants to stop for a minute. She had no idea this would be so exciting and so scary. She wants to stop her bike and close her eyes. She wants to see if she can feel if Merle is close.

"Hey," says Roland. "We're there. Don't stop now."

"I just needed to catch my breath," says Bunny, wishing he would be quiet. How can she concentrate if he is always talking? The sun feels nice on her face.

"Buster is happy," says Roland. "I think he can smell the river."

The hill is steep and they keep their brakes on all the way down. But she can see they are almost somewhere.

"Is this New Hope?" she asks but he shakes his head.

"We're still in New Jersey. New Hope is the other side of the river. There's a bridge up there," says Roland, pulling over and stopping on the sidewalk. "You want to go across and start looking or get some food first? Thirsty?"

"I was kind of planning on going alone," says Bunny. It is hard to talk because it is hard to breathe. "But I can meet you later maybe." The town is pretty and everywhere she looks there are sweet little houses, everything looks so old and nice.

"Oh, hey. That's okay. I get it. I'll hang back. Don't worry." Roland nods a lot of times.

"I don't want to hurt your feelings or anything," she says.

"Don't worry about it. I'll hang around here and catch you later. Lots of luck." He is busy with Buster now, fussing with him and lifting him out of the basket into his arms. "Me and Buster have a river to see," he says. "Don't we, boy."

"Wait. I have to be wearing this." She reaches into her knapsack and pulls out the scarf.

"Little hot for that, isn't it?" Roland looks puzzled.

"No, it's just right." Bunny smiles, putting it around her neck. Next she unpacks her jacket. The one jacket she embroidered. Merle's name on one pocket and Bunny's on the other. She puts it on, her back to Roland. She feels very close to Merle, very warm. Merle is here somewhere, she just knows it. Everything is going to be okay.

"Hey," says Roland. "That's very nice work. Did you do that yourself? Check out those rays." Roland is looking at the back of the jacket, a sunburst, a rainbow, shooting stars, you name it.

"Most of it," she answers. "Some of it. My sister did the back. I did the front." She turns around to show him her name on one pocket, Merle's on the other. A vine of flowers going up by the buttons on one side, and by the buttonholes on the other. It is really beautiful.

"You said your sister's name was Honey-Lou," says Roland. "Was your sister's name Merle?" asks Roland. His face looks so funny. "Merle Cunningham? That wasn't your sister, was it?" He is standing there with his dog in his arms, his bike leaning against a post.

Bunny doesn't feel like answering, and her hand goes up to cover Merle's name. "I don't have to answer everything you ask me. I didn't ask you what your mother's name was."

"Carol."

"Carol. I don't care what her name is. I don't even know you."

"Was your sister Merle Cunningham, Bunny?" Roland's voice sounds so kind. It really makes her mad.

"Shut up!" Bunny surprises herself by screaming. There are people walking on the sidewalks but not so many. It is still early in the morning. A few of them stop to look at Bunny. "Just shut up! Why are you so nice! I hate you! And that stupid dog is going to die!" Bunny lets her bike fall right over on the sidewalk.

Roland's face turns bright red. He kisses the top of Buster's head.

"I know that," he whispers.

MOMMA WAS SHAKING and she had a paper sack in her arms.

Bunny put her fingers in her ears. "I don't believe you. I don't believe you." She didn't raise her voice at all. She spoke calmly. "I don't believe you. You're lying."

"Believe it," screamed Momma, emptying a sack of what Bunny at first thought was trash on the table. "Believe it." Bunny picked up Merle's sewing things, many twists of colored thread, her tiny manicure scissors. Her jacket. Unfinished. "They found this. It was hers. Here. You take it." Momma pushed everything into Bunny's arms. "What do I want this shit for!"

BUNNY IS STILL crying. She's on the bridge now. She stands there where she had planned to stand, wearing the jacket. She stands in the middle of the green bridge under the blue sky, above the blue water of the Delaware River. She imagines the little ballpoint X up in the sky over her head. Cars pass and make that humming sound on the metal grid. The bridge is like a big musical instrument. It tickles to stand here, it makes your feet tickle like crazy. Bunny leans her arms on the rail and she looks into the water, which is beautiful. A whole bunch of kids are climbing around on the grassy banks with fishing poles. There is a fat lady with cherries on her hat standing next to a tall man. Bunny is making those hiccuping sounds that come from so much crying. She looks to her right, toward New Hope, but she doesn't see anyone. She looks up in the sky, which is also beautiful. Just like Merle said. She looks back at Roland. He is waving and waving.

HERB'SPAJAMAS

RUDY CERVANTES DIED by my back door and although I am sorry for his death there is nothing I could have done to save him. Not even if I denied him the little bit of pleasure we'd both grown used to. Still, it's the worst that happened so far. Rudy was a good soul but he smoked. I tried that once, choked, and let my body tell me something, but Rudy liked his cigarette after the act of love and since I forbade smoking in the bedroom, he'd generally light up in the kitchen and sit in the back hall, by the service elevator. You could hear the wind whistle down the shaft sometimes, and this made him feel peaceful enough to go home. One time he said he wished he could stay all the way through to breakfast and after. But we knew that wasn't in the cards. We never wanted to worry May. We never meant for her to have to let on that she knew, if she did know. If she woke up and missed him sometimes she never said so.

But he died. It was such a surprise.

We had had a fine time as always and he'd said he was coming back for another half hour after he had his Winston. I waited and fell asleep, draping the sheet over my thigh the way that makes me look most delicious due to the path the moon takes on my bed, and when I woke it was three-thirty. I turned to look at the clock, and no Rudy. It wasn't like him not to say good-bye and besides there were his trousers neatly folded on the back of the chair, and in that moment I knew something had happened to the sweetest of men. I put on my bathrobe and slippers and I even combed my hair, knowing what I would find, and I wanted to be dressed respectfully because there was no reason for Rudy not to be either in my bed or his own except that death had claimed him. Then I drew a deep breath and walked the narrow hall to the kitchen. And outside my door there was Rudy, sitting on the floor, the cigarette still in his fingers holding a tremendously long ash. He must have died instantly and slid down the wall like an ice-cream cone melting. He looked so natural there. But he didn't look lifelike; I knew he was dead. The real Rudy would have looked up from being aware of my perfume, but this Rudy didn't stir. It made tears spring to my eyes to see him like that, my heart nearly stopped on its own. "Oh Rudy," I whispered, "already I am missing you," and as if in answer I heard the wind start to kick up in the elevator shaft. Poor Rudy, I felt of him then and his hands and face were cold but he wasn't stiff anywhere, if you get my drift, really I just wanted to say good-bye to every part of him, Rudy would have understood that I think. He was wearing Herb's pajama top, which I always made him do. "Do you want to catch your death of cold," I would say to him. So he would compromise with the top half. It didn't catch fire from his cigarette either; Herb was a nut for inflammable. I sat with him for a while, I don't know how long, staring at the gray doors of the service elevator, listening to the pipes clank. I took the cigarette from between his poor fingers and put it in my pocket. Oh Rudy, I wondered, was it the smoking that got you? If he was ill he kept it from me. If his heart pounded unevenly, if his hands tingled, if his head ached or his bowels ran red, he never spoke of it. Rudy was not a man to complain. I touched my lips to his cool forehead.

I must have seen Rudy a thousand times before I noticed him.

"Well, I noticed you, Belle," he told me. "I noticed you the first time you bought in those low-slung silver slippers with the back strap."

"Oh those," I replied, laughing, thinking we had forever. "I was young then."

"You're young now," said Rudy, moving my hand to show me where I was young.

Well, it doesn't do to think of these things anymore.

So Rudy's time had come and if it was to be I was glad enough it was after a night of love instead of the third floor while May snored away and he stared at patterns of car lights on the ceiling. Still, it was a predicament. I never made a secret of my life but neither did I broadcast it, and we never meant to harm May in any way or rub her nose in it, as it were. But the truth is, May had never cared for the act of love; her favorite was a box of jelly doughnuts whereas I, as they say, could not seem to tire of it. Even at my age, which was sixty. Rudy had shown up at my front door one midnight and that was the start of it. "I saw your light," he said. I keep a lamp burning in my front window. "You know what I like about you, Belle?" Rudy used to say to me. "What, Rudy," I'd answer. "You're old, like me," he'd say and we'd laugh, although these lines were not original with Rudy; I had read them somewhere myself in the pages of a magazine. But you can't put a padlock on humor. And while I'm old I know a few things and my form is just as nice as ever it was, not having been weighed down by childbearing and always being supported by the best foundation garments money can buy. May is a lot younger but, as I said, not much interested in things of the flesh to do with Rudy.

Anyway, here was my dilemma. There was a dead husband outside the apartment and he wasn't mine. I had to return him to his own door. This presented a problem since I am barely five feet four and Rudy himself was not a big man but there is some truth to the term dead weight. Rudy alive I think I could have carried up to the roof joyfully if he had asked me to, such is the power of love, but Rudy dead was another matter. There was no breath in him, nothing to buoy him up. The fact is, I could not move Rudy one inch myself. On top of that I knew that bodies began to freeze in their positions and I wasn't sure how much time I had.

There was no one for me to turn to except Edith, and I didn't want to scare her with a ringing phone this hour of the night, seeing as how her apartment is so big around her, but dawn was fast approaching and Rudy needed to be on the third floor in less than an hour. When she picked up the phone I didn't tell her exactly what was wrong, but I said, "Edith, it's me, Belle. I need you to come here on the double-quick. It's a matter of life and death. No time for questions. Don't make a sound." Edith has such a good heart that she was here in no time, with her hair in those pink rubber curlers and wearing a huge white nightgown with tiny roses on it. Edith is a big woman. I was waiting at the door and said right off, "Sit down, Edith. Rudy's dead in the back hall. He died here tonight smoking a cigarette." Edith patted her curlers.

"What?" she said.

"You heard me. It's true. And we've got to get him out of here before the whole world wakes up," I said, pointing meaningfully downward as if to indicate the third floor. Edith did not move. I pulled her into my kitchen and sat her down at the table. I brought her the apricot brandy, which is helpful at moments like this, and Edith took two swallows. "I am suffering from toothache," she said. "My teeth don't meet and I can't even bite bread." She had lost the thread of our conversation.

"Rudy is dead," I reminded her. "I asked you to come."

"Oh no." She began to cry.

"We're running out of time," I said. I have known Edith since she moved here, in 1953. I knew her mother. I pointed out that May would hate to find her husband had died in another woman's apartment and that woman me. I know Edith could never approve of the way I lived my life. She would not want to be a party to my affairs. But I was not asking for approval here, I was asking for help. "Come with me," I said. "We have to get him out of here."

At first Edith was nervous as a kitten since she had probably never set eyes on a naked man, let alone a dead one. But I reminded her Rudy wasn't naked. He was wearing Herb's pajamas. So we opened the back door holding hands and we looked at the poor man together. I didn't feel like saying anything. He looked different already in the five minutes I'd been gone. His fingers were blue and his poor eyes looked sunken. "I've brought Edith to help," I said, as if he could still hear, and Edith began to tremble. "It's all right, " I said, and touched her large shoulder. "I'm talking to myself."

Edith patted her curlers again. "Oh dear, oh dear," she said, which sounded old-fashioned, but Edith is old-fashioned. Her favorite actor is Fred Astaire. Then Edith said, "He isn't dressed, Belle."

I said, "Well, not in his street clothes, Edith."

"Does he have anything on under that shirt?" she asked, and I had to say I wasn't sure. I wasn't. I couldn't remember. "Well, I can't touch him then, Belle, you know I have never even seen that thing." She wouldn't go nearer until I'd assured her he was wearing his underpants. I prayed the Lord that he was and I was right. Poor Rudy. He wore red checked boxer shorts that May bought for him by the dozen from her sister-in-law, who got them cheap. But Rudy never minded. He was a saint among men. All during this time I was moaning, which was not like me at all, and wiping away the tears. Then Edith said, "Oh, Belle, I can't touch him. He's dead."

And I said, "Well, of course he's dead, Edith. That's why I called you here."

"We have to call the police," she said, starting to tremble again.

"What is May going to say when she wakes up and can't find her Rudy, and it turns out he's here outside my door, and I'm your oldest friend in the building? Do you think you'll be on the Chrysanthemum Committee?" Well, I hated to hurt her where she lived but I had no choice. We were running out of time. May is the head of the gardening club, although she never lifts a trowel.

"Maybe if I get under his arms," said Edith then, and somehow with a scooping motion she did and we managed to get him over her shoulder, his poor thin legs hanging down. He was stiffening up a bit, and she kept imagining his manhood against the small of her back but I said it was just the buttons on Herb's pajamas, although I was not positive myself. Rudy was a fine man for one so short. It was awkward getting down the stairs, but the weight was no problem for Edith, who is nearly six feet nothing and weighs one hundred and ninety pounds. She cried the whole way, in tiny little mews.

"Shhh," I kept saying.

"I can't shhh," she said. "I am carrying a dead person. I am carrying a dead man." *Mew mew.* I wanted to point out it wasn't just any dead man, it was Rudy Cervantes, who had repaired our shoes for thirty years, but I was feeling too bad myself to bring this up.

"Don't trip on your nightgown," I said.

And Edith managed beautifully. Down the flight of stairs, across the tiles to 3C, while I tiptoed behind her, praying no dog would start barking, and that the papers would not be delivered early. Edith is strong. She could chop her own wood if she had to. She could haul her own water. And she carried Rudy Cervantes to his own front door, and let him slide down her back to a sitting position on the floor. Then the trouble was he was still wearing

Herb's pajamas. I couldn't think of anything to do but take them off. That left Rudy in his boxers but it couldn't be helped. I gave him a kiss on top of his cold head. "I hope I don't burn in hell for my part in this," Edith said and then she went home. And so did I. Thank God the early risers in the building were miraculously asleep and so were the Mexicans who sing all night. But I have given love freely and sometimes God cuts me a little slack.